Beltane

LENORA HENSON

Copyright © 2014 Lenora Henson

All rights reserved.

ISBN: 0615953654
ISBN-13: 978-0615953656

DEDICATION

For The Mighty Oak.

ACKNOWLEDGMENTS

Special thanks to cover model RaeChelle Leiken. You are simply divine RaeRae. Thanks to my soul sisters Joanna DeVoe and Dawn Champine. You inspire me daily. Thanks to Michelle Galyon and Celena Moulton. We've come full circle ladies. Thank you to the women of Psyche's Circle for your wild awesomeness. Thank you to Jennifer Adele for your support and friendship. Thank you to Janice McNutt for the photo shoot locations. The poppies never cease to delight. Hearty huge thanks to the readers, who keep me perpetually motivated and enthused. Thank you to Sophia and Jack, who remind me to laugh and lighten up when I become too serious about the writing/editing process. Thank you to Jessica Jernigan for your friendship, support and knowledge. Thank you to Jim Murphy... for everything.

PROLOGUE

Scotland, Early 1600s

There was an aura of quiet panic in the dense Scottish forest. The world was eerily still. Even the trees dared not move their boughs, though the breeze was brisk. The birds stilled their wings and the rodents waited in their holes. Magic was afoot. It could be sensed.

A handsome young man, aristocratic and dangerous, sat astride a black horse. He sneered and contemplated the girl's flight. *She's faster than I gave her credit for–or she's used sorcery to escape again,* he thought. By the time he fully realized he had just killed the oldest healer in the land, the young girl had disappeared from sight.

Witch!

Oh she is a devil, that girl! William grimaced, his face filled with pure contempt for Mage. She was the most stubborn female he'd ever come across–and he had come across many in his twenty-two years. She'd fought him from the moment he'd seen her red hair blazing in the ambivalent Scottish sun.

"How dare either one of ye curse me? Ye filthy heretics," he grumbled.

He looked back onto the path, and then slung his bow back in place with shaking hands. *Oh, what I will do to that girl when I find her*, he steamed. He'd murder her himself this time. It's what his father would want him to do–to finish what he'd started and make sure the wicked woman was eliminated and cast into hell. *How dare she defy me?*

There was no way he could let the town people know she had survived the burning or there would be more trouble. She was a true witch, and he knew no end to her power. He'd have to dispose of her himself, God help him. He bowed his head. She was with child. Possibly his. She was just barely showing. A guilty dread took hold of his chest. It was momentary, but everlasting.

He brushed the feeling away, and made his intentions clear.

The witch has to die.

And then it occurred to him again that he'd already killed one very powerful witch, and she had cursed him. The words were still fresh in his ears.

Violence and shame, ye have sewn
violence and shame ye shall beget
Your children's children shall not be redeemed
until my child's children are redeemed.
So mote it be.

An overwhelming fear, tight and terrifying rippled through his being. He turned back to the old woman, whose heart had been shot through by his arrow.

William was startled, realizing the crone was not

alone. The witch's limp, lifeless body lay still in the spot where he'd killed her, but another woman was kneeling by her side, aiming some sort of unusual device at the crone's wound. The device flashed light and made a quick clicking sound.

More witchcraft! William determined.

This new witch also had red hair, and it was piled on top of her head. She wore the most peculiar garments. *What kind of demon visits me now?* Suddenly he began to feel the full weight of the curse that had been brandished only moments before. It was all happening so fast! He couldn't breathe. He felt strangled.

He feared his unborn child.

The strange woman looked straight at him and spoke. "You're running out of time, you lily-livered cur. This has gone on a few centuries too long for my liking. You'll have to deal with me now. Visit the Wicked Garden if you'd like to know the wrath of Miss Poni," the woman barked.

She raised her hand, and William felt something odd pass through his chest. Before he could even unsling his bow, the woman faded away before his eyes. Was he having visions now? The crone had surely cursed him good. He breathed a short-lived sigh of relief after the demon had retreated, until he then realized the crone was gone too.

Confused, he scanned the area in every direction, his horse doing half circles to follow his frantic lead. The forest looked empty, but it didn't *feel* empty. He gazed back down at the spot where blood had spilled. She was truly gone! In place of the dead body was a flat stone engraved with an unusual knot.

William heard a growl from the woods. He saw fierce eyes, and a wild creature stepped forward showing its incisors. Hundreds of tiny lights twinkled in the shadows.

Fae? Could the legends be true?

One of the lights morphed into a stunning black haired beauty. William was captivated, entranced by her mystical aura.

"Did ye understand the curse lad?" the ravishing creature asked.

William shook his head *no* as a new terror took hold.

The fairy smiled. William thought there was something sinister and self-serving in her grin. And she told him: "It means there'll be no rest'n fer the wicked."

∞

Mage tore through the forest as quick as her long legs would move her. She was a fast girl, always had been. She could outrun most boys in the countryside, and it was serving her well as she maneuvered through the maze of trees. She had to get to the water and soon. She had to get to Reid.

Suddenly a light flashed bright before her eyes, and sent her headfirst into a blanket of dirty, rotting leaves. She dug her palms out of the muck, and wiped at her face with a forearm, covering her natural beauty with dirt and grime. She felt her belly, and sensed the baby. She was fine.

Mage cautiously looked about, on guard to attack or be attacked. She heard a rustling of footsteps, and then, as if time was bending, the fairy stood before her.

Claire.

"I have a gift, Mage."

"I've no time fer pleasantries Claire, he's comin' fer me," Mage hissed, her voice hoarse and her lungs burning from the run.

Mage had grown up with the fae. Claire was her friend, and she typically would have spent an evening such as this enjoying her company. But this was not a typical evening, and she felt she was not in any position to be enjoying anything ever again.

She made to flee, but Claire blocked her path with a massive diaphanous wing that flickered gorgeous colors of green, aqua and magenta from the last of the dusk's sunrays that filtered through the forest ceiling.

"It's from yer Grand Mama. She had me fetch it from the village."

"Hurry!" Mage cried a half whisper, half yelp.

"First this," Claire handed her a silver Quaich. Reid had given it to Mage earlier that year. She was tempted to wax nostalgic on the evening he'd gifted it, but there was no time for lovely reminiscing.

Mage felt a small pang of hope that she might soon be reunited with her love, and she quickly tucked the silver cup into her bag. "And what else have ye got, Claire? Hurry!"

Claire held out her graceful hands. A square box materialized. A chaotic Celtic knot was beautifully, meticulously carved into each panel. "This was nah made by anyone from the village," Mage stated.

"Nah. Theo crafted the box fer ye," Claire smiled brightly.

Mage thought about her best friend, Claire's brother. The thought of never seeing him again nearly brought her to her knees. "Hand it o'r," she managed to creak.

"Whit's *inside* was fetched from the village," Claire said.

Mage took the box, and instantly felt an overwhelming sense of sadness, pain and shame. She closed her eyes, and could see what was inside. She gasped for breath.

"How could ye? How could ye give me such a thing?" Mage whispered, tears racing down her face.

"It is a gift."

"It is a curse!"

"Aye, and had ye not started one ye couldn't finish we'd not be in this trouble, would we now? Take it!"

Mage took the box. She hastily stuffed it into her bag. Then she looked around the wildwood, making sure she had another moment to spare. "Why would ye give me such a thing?"

"It holds great power. Magic from all yer ancestors was put into the making of this box. They're watching over ye, the old ones are. From the trees and the sky and water and the especially the fire. They offer aid."

"I donnae mean the bloody box! I mean whit's inside! Why would ye give me such a thing? It's my punishment," Mage cried.

For a moment she thought she could see a tinge of compassion or remorse in Claire's eyes, but then it passed. It was not her way.

"It is your salvation," the fairy replied.

"It is a reminder of my eternal damnation!"

"According to *his* beliefs, but suit yerself," Claire countered.

"How do I open it then?" Mage growled.

Claire reached out and touched the large amethyst pendant that sat against Mage's heart. "Forgive yerself."

Tears rolled again, this time even harder. Mage ripped the amethyst from her neck and flung it into the forest. She let loose a throaty banshee wail: "Never!"

Claire covered her ears to protect herself from the witch's deafening scream, and when the screaming stopped, the girl was gone.

"Whit's fur ye'll no go by ye," the fairy whispered solemnly and disappeared into the ether.

The wheel will turn, and turn, and turn.
Violence and shame will be the fate of
their descendants,
generation after generation.
The water will take them under.
It will take their daughters,
and they will not be redeemed.
Even when the water takes them,
they will not be redeemed.

Then the huntress will have a son,
and her son will have two loves.
The first will be a girl with hair as dark as blood
and scars that go deep beneath the surface.
He will give her the stone that saves her,
and she will give him despair.
When he finds the stone again,
He will find his heart,
and all may be redeemed.

The first and the second and the psychopomps
will follow the Horned God to the underworld.
Amethyst is the key that will open the buried box.
When the spirits are set free,
all will be redeemed.

Look to the twenty-first to find the second.
Find her, and all shall be redeemed.

Part One

Irvine, 1920s

A familiar and delectable aroma welcomed Epona as she entered the cottage's sun porch. The nine-year-old's face broke into a wide, wild grin. Freckles practically popped off her sunburnt cheeks. She dashed into the kitchen and then, suddenly mindful of her footwear, came to a halt. She'd just finished chores, which included the tending of her horse. Her little work boots were filthy.

She scampered back to the porch, and as she removed the boots she stared with jubilant eyes at the long farm table that sat between the kitchen and living room. A beautifully crafted strawberry shortcake was the centerpiece. It was her mama's specialty, and Epona was determined to learn how to make one just as tasty and pretty one day.

She quickly scanned the rest of the table. It was covered with Mason jars of strawberry jam. Her mama had finished the last batch that afternoon. There were also baskets ready to be filled. It was a Summer Solstice tradition. Every farmhand at Snyder Farms would receive a basket of fresh strawberries, several jars of strawberry jam, shortcake and fresh cream. It was Epona's favorite time of year. Even the heat couldn't deter her from enjoying the festive week.

She took stock of her surroundings. The cottage was quiet, hot and miserable. She pulled out a handkerchief, wiped her sweaty brow, and listened for activity. She was good at listening. She could hear and see more than most people. The sight was second nature for her, and she still couldn't quite understand how the rest of the world, or what little she knew of it, was not as sensitive.

She listened closer and heard a distant repetitive hum.

"Mama?" Epona called.

A quick search of the main floor and the upstairs dormers turned up empty.

"Mama?" she called out again. She stilled herself and listened. The hum continued. With more urgency in her step, she moved to the cottage basement. She let out a sigh of relief as she saw the flicker of candlelight, but then she instantly felt a burning in her belly and her body tensed. The energy in the basement was dark and dense and electric. The temperature was cooler, yes, but it was heavy. Epona sensed an otherworldly unfolding.

Magic.

"Mama?" she whispered.

The hum had been a chant.

Epona walked toward a corner of the basement where candlelight was cast under a door. She clenched her hands and held her breath. She despised that corner space. It was a tiny blocked-off room where something quite sinister and horrendous resided. Epona's mother,

Carlin, had warned her never to enter into that room. *Ever.*

And Epona hadn't by choice. Her father, Colin Ferguson III, had locked her in the room once when she was five-years-old. Just once. Epona thought she might not survive the two-hour confinement. The energy practically burned her from the inside out. She had been locked in complete darkness. She hadn't a clue what was in the room with her.

She wasn't far from the door when she stopped and heard her mama's voice. Carlin was chanting a spell. She was trying to work magic on whatever sinister object resided inside the horrible room.

Epona was a strong girl, perhaps one of the strongest, but not in that moment. Crocodile tears rolled down her freckled face.

"Mama?" she whimpered. Epona knew better than to interrupt a spell, but she was terrified, and not just for herself, but her mama. She closed her eyes and a not too uncommon vision came to pass again: *she saw her mama drowning in the cottage lake.* She had been seeing this vision since she was a tiny thing. Carlin had always dismissed the visions with a nervous wave of her hand, and an obvious catch in her throat.

The hum got louder, and more intense.

"Mama!" Epona screamed.

The door to the tiny room flung upon and Carlin Fitzgerald fell out onto the cellar floor. She was sweating and panting.

"Mama!" Epona cried.

Epona fell to her mother, lifted her gently and supported her weight. She brushed the sweaty, matted hair out of her face. Once her mother was breathing easier, Epona dared a glance into the foreboding room. Sitting on a small table was an old box, carved meticulously with a beautiful Celtic knot.

"Mama, I've ruined your magic," she began to cry.

Carlin shook her head. "No. No. No, Poni. There is no magic strong enough to do what I am trying to do."

Epona looked at her queerly. "And what exactly are ye trying to do, Mama? That box is evil. Can't ye feel the torment?"

Carlin nodded a quick agreement. Just being in proximity to the box was rendering her weak as a kitten. She pulled herself up. A quick swipe from her apron, and her red, sweaty face lost its sickening glisten. "Aye. It be a cursed object fer sure. And it's been haunting our family fer too long. I was trying to open it, Poni. I was trying to fix this mess once and fer all, but I'm not capable. I've been trying fer ten years to open the bloody thing and I cannae do it!"

"And what do ye suppose we have to gain by open'n something so horrible, Mama?" Poni asked, trying to put courage back into her words, but failing miserably.

Carlin sighed. She went to the box, and touched it. Her hand instantly jerked back. "Come here child."

"I will not!" Epona stood steadfast in her spot.

To her utter despair, Carlin picked up the box. Epona could tell it was shocking her all the while. She brought it to Epona. "Touch it... Just a fingertip will do."

Epona's finger trembled, as she reluctantly reached out and tapped the box. It burnt her finger. The energy was beyond her worst nightmare. She covered her face.

"Please don't make me touch it again, Mama." She peeked her eyes open and Carlin had set the box down. Epona stared at the knotted design. "Mama, I've seen the knot. I've seen it in mah dreams and in mah visions."

"I've no doubt ye have, Poni. Did ye see a key by chance or where a key might fit?"

Epona indicated that she had not.

Carlin sighed. "It's got to go. I cannae have it in mah house any longer, and I cannae keep trying futile attempts at open'n a box that isn't meant to be opened– not yet any way. It'll be gone by the end of the Solstice, and ye'll have no need to fear it anymore, at least until yer older. It'll be for ye and yer kin to deal with then. Do ye hear me, child? Ye got to stay strong, Poni. We're *all* counting on ye."

"The old ones?" Epona asked.

Carlin gave a thin-lipped nod. "Aye child, the old ones, and the ones to come. Ye got to hold on fer us all."

Epona stood up tall and straight. "Oh I will, Mama. I will."

"And promise me child, promise me one thing," Carlin said.

"Yes, Mama?"

"Above all else, Poni, ye got to keep yer mind yer own."

Whit's fur ye'll no go by ye.

CHAPTER ONE

Irvine, 2010s

Poppies. There were lots and lots of gloriously orange poppies. The image burned in Gretchel's psyche, and it was the only thing she remembered as she came back to consciousness. She'd passed out between the cottage floor and Eli's arms after seeing the legendary birthmark on the ass of one of the world's greatest and most controversial storytellers.

Poppies.

The orange flowers were the only things she could see.

Eyes blinking rapidly, she pulled herself up onto her elbows. Her eyes finally focused, and she saw more poppies still. But these poppies were in the painting she had created so many years ago. It hung on the living room wall in the cottage. It was the Wicked Garden, of that she knew for sure. That damned place would forever be the source of her anguish. She released a deep breath, but it did little to comfort her.

Something new was becoming her center of

attention. Humans. Two people with very curly hair hovered above. Her eyes shifted focus from the poppies to the owners of the faces. *Eli. Oh sweet Eli. My one and only.* And the other... Her eyes squinted as she desperately tried to comprehend who this person was.

"Are you Pan?" she finally whispered coyly.

The man, who was born Graham Odysseus Duncan, returned her question with a nod of his head and an immense smile. "I am Pan," he said curtly.

She looked at Eli. "That makes you The Messenger."

And she lost consciousness. Again.

∞

The next day Eli stomped stark raving mad into his parent's sprawling hotel suite. "I cannot *believe* you said 'I am Pan!' Seriously Dad, just what in the hell is wrong with you?" Eli ranted.

The man formally known as Peter Stewart smiled broadly. "Son, there is not, nor has there ever been anything wrong with me. I am an *as-is* kind of fella. Don't burden me with your restricted perceptions."

Eli shook his head ferociously, and paced the living area. There was no use reprimanding someone to whom the scolding took no hold. Eli flung a sofa pillow across the suite. He liked throwing things. It was a powerful release. And with that release he reluctantly gave up the fight.

"She's fine now, Dad. She's a bit star-struck of course, and has a goose egg on her head from the first fall, but she's fine. As we speak, both she and Ame are making an obsessive list of questions to ask you about your latest book, which is, of course, *Pan's Rebirth*. Do you have any idea what a mind-fuck this is for them?"

Graham smiled thoughtfully and stroked his long, out-of-control beard. "If I recall correctly, *you* were the one who wanted them to know my true identity. How I delivered the news is my business. And *Pan's Rebirth* is my masterpiece. You know it's been number one on the *New York Times Bestsellers List* since it came out this spring. That tells me this country is hungry for something. They're hungry for the wild and the wise. They want to enter that sacred forest of the Divine No-No. They can instinctually feel it is really a *yeah-yeah* and they're ready for someone to give them permission to camp out under the stars of their own original thought, bivouac style. Free mind. Open heart. Fresh air. Permission is granted my loves! Permission is granted!"

He marched to the verandah and bellowed to the masses congregated in the courtyard for a lunch of Cobb salad and snobby soufflé. "Go forth my beautiful, wild ones. Pan and the Wild Mother are waiting with open arms!"

Diana surfaced from the suite's bedroom to witness Graham's exuberant call to action. Eli gave her an imploring look, silently begging her to stop the spectacle.

She waved him off. She'd lived with the madness for over forty years. "Let him do his thing."

Eli rolled his eyes, sent a prayer to the residents of Irvine and again, granted Graham his personal freedom. Though it might not have been such an issue if Graham had been wearing clothes. Eli expected the front desk to be ringing any minute.

The phone indeed rang, and Diana quickly made peace with unquestionable authoritative experience. It was routine at this point. The naked subpoena was her husband's signature dish.

She hung up the phone, snapped her fingers and sharply motioned for Eli to sit at the small dining table. He complied. Diana pulled out two tablets: one paper, one electronic. She uncapped the top of a very expensive pen and addressed her son in business-like manner.

"We have decided that Gretchel may inform her immediate family of Graham's identity, under the strict condition that she cast a spell swearing them to secrecy. I assume she's capable of that kind of magic?" Diana peered above her bifocals, eyeballing her son with the rhetorical question.

Eli shrugged. He had no idea what kind of magic Gretchel was capable of, other than she'd bewitched him beyond repair.

"Ame is free to change her last name to Duncan if she so chooses."

"And me?" Eli inquired

"You're a grown man, Elliot. You've been free to change your name since you were eighteen. Grow up already."

Eli raged. He clenched his fists, and cursed his mother silently. *Both* his parents were the epitome of the mind-fuck. Self-serving pragmatists.

It had been revealed just the day before that his mother was wrong about Eli having another love awaiting him. The second love of his life was his daughter, Ame. Diana had shown remorse, but it was short-lived. She had already defaulted back to her pushy persona.

"Okay. It's time to dive into the depths of Gretchen's abyss," the tiny women declared.

"It's Gretchel…" Eli sighed.

"It's Persnickety Possum for all I care."

Eli froze himself in a dubious stare.

"Let's move on, Elliot. What did Gretch-el mean by you were *The Messenger* last night?"

Eli ran both hands through his thick curls, like he always did when he was frustrated, confused or on the edge. "I'm dad's messenger boy. I must have told her at some point. She calls me Hermes. I don't know, Mother. Is it really important?"

"Oh, I think it is very important," Diana assured her son.

"Then you ask her," Eli replied sternly.

"Oh I will. She doesn't scare me."

She should, Eli thought.

"So what kind of crazy are we looking at?" Diana asked in her typical just barely above the freezing mark tone.

Eli was incredulous. "I thought Miss Poni's testimony eluded to Gretchel not being mentally ill, but cursed, haunted and/or possessed."

"Elliot, she is all of those things and more as far as I can tell. As a transpersonal psychologist I can also tell you that she suffers from a multitude of mental ailments. If I had to guess from only knowing her a day I would say that her post-traumatic stress is beyond severe. This woman is a walking time bomb."

"You don't have to be so aggressive. She's not out

to get you. She's just very defensive about her past. It's not that she doesn't want to be fixed, but she wants to do it her way."

"Sounds just like an alcoholic or addict, probably both. Tell me what you know," she responded arrogantly, and pressed record on her video camera.

CHAPTER TWO
Irvine, 2010s

Eli started from the beginning, some Diana knew, some she didn't. All of it was intriguing. Now that Diana knew the woman was a descendant of the Solstice Twins, she was completely fascinated by her, but she still couldn't bring herself to *like* her after what she'd done to Eli.

The low down: Gretchel had third degree burns on the right side of her torso, which Eli had always assumed were caused by the accident in the truck that was in the Wicked Garden. Why the truck was still there he didn't know. The scar on her forehead, the cigarette lighter scars on her abdomen and the knife scar on her stomach were all caused by Troy, and Eli assumed many of the others were too. Gretchel had been a self-mutilator, and there were nineteen cuts, all the same length, in two rows of seven and one of five, on the left side of her torso, that she had inflicted on herself.

"Nineteen... Very interesting," Diana commented.

Diana already knew that the accident involving

Gretchel's father occurred when she was thirteen. Eli confided that Gretchel had been pregnant twice as a teenager. Eli remembered Gretchel saying one child had been beat out of her, but by whom he was not certain. He also noted that she had been involved with a twenty-two-year-old at the age of twelve.

"What do you know about Gretchel's father?" Diana asked.

Eli knew very little, other than he was an alcoholic, and had turned on her at some point. Eli reported that Gretchel had been very close with her father, but she claimed to have been victim of his abuse after she reached puberty. Something had happened.

She admitted trying to commit suicide twice after the accident, both by drowning, he assumed. Gretchel had spent time in a psych-ward after the second attempt, but Eli didn't know the duration or where. Gretchel claimed Teddy magically pulled her out of her catatonic daze.

Diana found this fact rather important, and made a note to keep her eye on the man. She was very aware that Teddy knew everything. She smelled the secrets emanating from his pampered skin.

Eli described Gretchel appearing anorexic in the pictures from Facebook, but had gained weight by the time he arrived in Irvine. He told Diana that when he was trying to persuade Gretchel to stay away from Troy during their Carbondale days, she continually told him she wasn't worth having. She was very adamant about her worth being zilch.

He told her that Troy had threatened to kill her and the baby when she was pregnant with Ame. Although he was not specific, he explained that Gretchel had accepted money from Troy during college in exchange for sex. He told his mother that during Gretchel's entire marriage a video had been used to blackmail her into submission and obedience. He had no idea the horror contained on the tape. He assumed it had something to do with sex. The tape was still missing.

Gretchel supposedly hadn't had sexual intercourse the last three years of her marriage, though he wasn't quite sure what had happened to cause the celibacy. During their marriage, Troy had locked her in their basement when she had attempted to paint a picture of Eli sailing away from her. "This fear of me leaving on a boat seems deep-rooted."

Graham suddenly looked up from his laptop. *The ship?* he wondered.

Eli went on to report that Gretchel was a bow-hunter. "She shot the buck that hangs in the cottage when she was twelve," he explained.

"There's a Horned God for ya," Graham smiled. Eli and Diana turned to him for a moment, and both promptly ignored the comment. Eli continued his deposition.

Eli told her what he knew about the voices, and that the Woman in Wool's modulation was stronger than the rest. He told her about the way her eyes looked empty when she was hearing them. He explained the nightmares, the rambling conversations he'd heard her have with herself a handful of times, the migraines, the sirens that sent her into flashbacks, the shattering of the bedroom mirror in which she possibly saw the Woman in Wool's reflection. He was also pretty sure Gretchel was trying to beat the demon with a pitching wedge the night he had returned to Irvine.

"You witnessed this psychotic collapse?"

"Yes. I've never seen anything so disturbing in my life," he remembered. "She was on top of the truck in the Wicked Garden. She was beating it mercilessly. When I called her name she looked to me, and then she looked back to the truck. It was as if her target disappeared once I had her attention."

"Why was she not hospitalized then? Why wasn't she put on medication?" Diana asked.

Eli shrugged. "I arrived while she was losing it, and she snapped out of it as soon as she was aware it was me. I heal her, Mom. I don't know how I do it, but my presence keeps her somewhat sane I guess."

"It's not your job to keep her sane. It is no one's job to help maintain the sanity of another human being. She needs to work through this," Diana retorted.

"I realize that, Mother. Maybe it was my job to keep her sane until the professional could help her."

No, Diana thought, *it's not my job either*.

"Do you know what triggered her breakdown the night you arrived?"

"Her son left for Chicago without notice. Zach went to stay with Troy's parents, whom Gretchel despises. And I just figured out why they treated Ame so horribly; they knew all along she wasn't Troy's child."

That sparked a new topic for Diana. "Speaking of Ame, she seems fairly well-adjusted considering her violent upbringing and her mother's condition. Although she's obviously extremely antagonistic."

"I'm pretty sure she gets that from you," Eli said

sourly.

Diana gave him a wooden stare, clearly not amused. Eli decided it would be best to continue.

"Ame's very intelligent, like Gretchel, but she's also incredibly intuitive. She's levelheaded, strong, focused and she wants so badly to protect her mother. In fact I know she's spent a good amount of energy mothering her mother. That's too much to ask from a child, especially one who has the potential to do great things. That's not biased is it?"

Diana softened. She sunk back in her chair, and cracked a small grin. Her eyes were warm and loving, which was completely out of character. "That's not biased, darling. Peter said you had a high opinion of Ame before you even knew she was your child. By the way, how couldn't you have known, Eli? Seriously?"

Eli fumed. The humility reached his face, and turned it bright red. He stood up to leave.

"I'm sorry... I'm sorry... I'm sorry!" Diana called out quickly. "Sit!"

Eli sat.

He cleared his throat of spite and continued. "My point is that Ame is okay. She doesn't seem to show any signs of mental illness or possession. But there are strange things going on at Snyder Farms, Mom. Last weekend Ame and her boyfriend tripped on 'shrooms... I had nothing to do with it, I swear!" Eli defended, as Diana shot him a disappointed if not disgruntled look. "Anyway, Ame freaked and jumped in the lake. I'd dreamt she was drowning only moments before it happened. Peyton and I were able to save her, but it was a close call. The lake is haunted just like the Wicked

Garden. I swear it is. When I told Gretchel what happened with Ame she was weirdly evasive, and all she would say is… 'She got to her.' We haven't talked about it since. I don't know exactly what I'm supposed to think or say."

Diana was scribbling quickly. *This is important. Very, very important,* she thought.

Graham put on a pair of plaid boxers, and came in closer to listen. "Was she insinuating the Woman in Wool got to her?" he asked.

Eli nodded.

"What do you make of this Peter?" Diana questioned.

"Darling, why don't you just call me Graham now?"

"Why don't you just answer my question?"

Graham snorted. "Sassypants," he cracked. "You say it was last weekend when they tripped? Last Saturday in fact?"

"Yes."

Graham stroked his wild beard, thinking, and what he thought was positively unbelievable even for him. *These two are definitely not ready to hear my take on the trip. I can hardly believe it myself.*

"Beats me love," he answered.

Diana looked at him funny. She quickly wrote down the information.

"What do you know about the other girl, Ame's cousin Holly?"

"Holly? Nothing really. She's sweet, quiet, reserved, respectful I suppose. She's pretty much the exact opposite of Ame."

"Yes... Yes she is," Diana stated with a sense of intrigue. She ran fingers through her *Anna Wintour*-esque hair as she considered the young girl's role.

"What's your point?" Eli asked.

She was thrown by the girl's mysteriousness. She tapped her custom-made pen on the table. "I don't know. I just felt a strange vibe from Holly. Anything else you can tell me?"

"Ame's very fond of horses like Miss Poni, but Gretchel hates them, she's afraid of them."

"Seriously?" Graham queried.

"Yeah, why?" Eli inquired. Graham raked through his beard some more, and shrugged. Eli continued, "Gretchel's childhood horse was a black mare named Pixie. She died the same year as the accident. Pixie is buried in the Wicked Garden. I remember Gretchel telling me, the last night I spent with her seventeen years ago, that she saw a horse in her dreams since she'd been pregnant. She also said she'd seen the ghosts in the garden. She said when she was awake she sometimes saw animals that others didn't see," Eli rambled, the recall of information rolling off his tongue with urgency.

"What kind of animals?"

Eli pressed his fingers to his temples, racking his brain to remember. "Lots of deer. I remember her saying she saw lots of deer."

"Any other animals?" Diana prodded. "Eli, animals are very symbolic. It's critical that you remember."

He lifted his head as the realization came to him, "A stag. She saw a stag and a snake."

"Anything else?"

"Yes. She said she mainly saw a wolf."

Graham's eyes lit up. "A wolf."

"A wolf," Eli repeated.

Diana dropped her pen and put a hand to her mouth. "What is it?"

"She's seeing Cernunnos. Cernunnos is the Horned God. He can shape-shift into these creatures," she whispered.

"The Horned God from the prophecy." Graham sought confirmation.

Diana shook her head a resounding *yes*. "How can this be? The prophecy says look to the twenty-first to find the second. Ame is not the twenty-first descendant. She is the twentieth. She is obviously the second love of Eli's life, but something is amiss."

Graham piped up. "Not really, darling. If she had two pregnancies before Ame, perhaps one of them was a girl."

"It would have to be a *living* descendant: a child that had been born. How can this be? How can she be the girl? And I still don't understand why Ame has that amulet! She's only the twentieth descendant," Diana reiterated. "Ame should be the twenty-first. It doesn't make sense. There has to be another girl out there," she looked at Eli carefully. "I think one of her children lived Eli, at least for a while. It would make the numbers add up. It would make Ame the twenty-first descendant."

Eli's face grew red again with rage. "No. No. No. She would have told me if she had given birth to another child."

Graham rolled his bright aqua eyes, and snorted again.

"Are you out of your freaking mind?" Diana yelled.

"You're just now finding out about your *own* damn child."

"She's right, kid," Graham interjected.

Diana persisted. "Is there anything more about her you can tell me, Eli? Anything that stands out to you?"

"Everything that woman does stands out to me!"

"She makes me stand out too," Graham whispered, crossing his legs.

Eli stared at the ceiling. Diana shook her head and pursed her lips.

"The doll," Eli whispered.

"What about a doll?"

"There's this old, ratty rag doll that she sleeps with. It's really kinda creepy."

Diana tapped at her lips with the pen. "And who did this doll belong to Eli, maybe a little girl? A child. Perhaps another daughter?"

Eli violently rubbed at his face and grabbed at his mane. "Little help here, Dad?"

"She could be right," Graham stated, siding with his wife yet again.

A round of the staring game quickly ensued between Eli and his mother.

Graham watched the virtual chess match, and thought he'd break the rules, as usual, by joining in. He stared back and forth between them until Eli cracked a smile. Graham spoke. "Look, we have no proof of another child right now, so there's no use bickering. What I want to know is: what is the extent of Aphrodite's mental illness?"

Diana tore her gaze away from her son, and took a deep breath. "The migraines, the flashbacks, the nightmares–they can all be attributed to post traumatic stress, that's obvious. The alcoholism, self-mutilation and anorexia are self-inflicted punishments, but also coping mechanisms, systematic to deeper issues. I'm sure they helped ease the anxiety, depression and irritability. She could have a borderline personality disorder. The truck accident traumatized her, possibly beyond repair, so I *need* to know the details to better diagnose.

"It seems as though when she put on the amethyst it provoked a sort of depersonalization disorder that worked an unheard of amount of time. She may have had this disorder when she came out of the psych-ward too. You mentioned that she *woke up* when she met Teddy. I'm captivated by the effect the jewel and the boy have had on her. It's fascinating. They both seem to possess a magic we don't yet understand.

"Gretchel not only has auditory hallucinations, but visual as well. She hears more than the one voice, in fact she hears many, and while that may sound like schizophrenia, it's complicated because she is aware of herself, of her own mind when she hears them. However, when she beat the truck she may have been following commands from the voice. It's very possible the voice commanded her during the suicide attempts as well. More often than not those voices don't stir when you are around, Eli. The nightmares are less prevalent too. You *do* have healing energy. You *are* special. You always have been, and there is a reason I spent years trying to keep you safe. This girl is the reason. This bloodline is the reason."

"Can she be helped, Mother? Without a mental

hospital?"

"That depends on her behavior. If she poses a physical threat to anyone including herself, I'll have her in a straightjacket quicker than Graham can raise his wand. I need to hear her story, Eli, and I need to hear the Solstice Twins' stories too."

"You heard Ella, they aren't talking, and I wouldn't cross them. As for Gretchel, if she won't open up to me, or Ame, then no one else stands a chance."

Diana picked up the pen, and tapped her lip again.

"Well you might want to remind her that unless she talks, the cycle of violence is going to continue and it continues with *your* daughter. How's that for motivation?"

"Quit stressing me out!" Eli cried.

"There may be one person that could get information out of her," Diana said, and glanced toward Graham.

"I know what you're thinking, and I won't let you manipulate her like that."

"It won't be manipulative if he's forthcoming with his intentions. Do you have a better idea? Of course you don't."

"I'll talk to her," Graham smiled. "I'm itching to get to know her better, but I won't report a thing back to you, my love, unless you relax, and put this obsessive aggression at ease. It reeks of egotism and duality. I wouldn't advise going into this with your battle gear on Diana; leave that for Gretchel."

"I was born wearing battle gear," the tiny woman with the sharp bob pronounced to her husband. Athenastyle. She closed her leather notebook and clicked her pen shut. The inquisition was over.

Thank gods, Eli thought.

Graham patted his son on the back, handed him the cap of his bottle of Perrier, and pointed to an umbrella stand. Without speaking, Eli took the cap and snapped it across the room, nailing his target with ease. The cap pinged, circled twice around and dropped to the bottom of the canister.

"My greatest talent," Eli moped.

Graham roared with jubilant laughter. "You light up my life, sweet boy!"

Diana rolled her eyes. "We're flying out this afternoon. A truck will be arriving later this week with my research. Find a place for us to stay indefinitely."

Eli grimaced. "What's the magic word, Mother?"

"*Now*," she smiled playfully. "I'll have my people take care of the furnishings and details."

The thought of his parents living so close set a whole new anxiety into motion. "Fine. I'll find you a house to stay *temporarily*, but please don't pressure Gretchel about anything until after prom and Beltane."

"A Beltane celebration?" Graham piped up, with a sparkle in his eyes.

"From what I understand it's a little milder than what you're accustomed to, Dad. There will be no nakedness. It's Ella's birthday celebration as well. You're both invited to the party next weekend at the cottage if you promise to behave yourselves."

"Pfffftt! You really are naive boy," Graham laughed.

CHAPTER THREE
Irvine, 2010s

Eli spent the following days desperately trying to convince Gretchel that Graham Duncan was his father, and that she had indeed met him. It was not an easy task, particularly since his parents had flown back to Oregon to prepare for an extended stay in Illinois before Gretchel had a chance to meet the man without fainting. She was under the impression that it was either a dream or she had reached a whole new level of lunacy.

Eli was struggling with his own sanity by midweek.

He'd had a lot to answer for, and Gretchel was ruthless in her interrogation until a day came when she stopped the harassment, and began internalizing the realization. She was processing. Eli allowed her the freedom, and quietly welcomed the silence.

Chew on that for a while. It was advice that Duncan had often suggested in his highly acclaimed and often admonished works of fiction. Gretchel was doing just that. Chewing. Processing. Chewing and processing.

Ame had returned to school, and began physical

therapy on her shoulder. Her future in volleyball was unclear, and she wasn't all that heartbroken, for she was hoping it would allow her more time to write. However, with prom preparations in full swing, her writing *still* wasn't given much priority.

They were also down to one car again, and Eli made a note to go car shopping. Ame had mentioned Gretchel wasn't nuts about the sedan anyway. She said her mother needed something big to suit her height and her personality. And Ame... Well Ame just needed to drive safer or to drive a car encased in bubble wrap perhaps.

By midweek, Eli was ready for Gretchel to start conversing again. He tried talking to her about the prophecy, and asked her to consider talking to his mother in a therapeutic environment. Gretchel firmly refused to even acknowledge his heartfelt recommendation.

"I have to finish this prom dress!" she shouted, and kicked him out of the studio that was temporarily *not* being used to paint, but was wall-to-wall fabric and notions.

A day then came when Gretchel decided it would be good for her to go into town–alone. Eli tried to prohibit their time apart, simply because he knew without him she might hear the voices, and possibly even see the Woman in Wool. But Gretchel was going stir-crazy with Eli constantly on her tail, and insisted she get out alone.

It was time. She needed a ton of essentials, and had a long shopping list for the Beltane celebration. She also had to pick up a necessity that she hadn't needed in three years. She assumed Eli would not want to make a tampon run.

She couldn't believe her cycle had returned and wasn't sure why it was now suddenly reemerging. As she drove into Irvine, she remembered her last cycle, and the torture she'd received that had caused it to stop.

The memory suddenly had a mind of its own, and she found herself driving through her old subdivision. She caught a glimpse of the house that she still technically owned, and where her torture had taken place. Her heart thumped wildly against her chest, and she felt more exposed than she had in months. She felt everyone in Irvine knew her secrets, and truth be told many of them did.

They know what ye did back then, lassie. We all do, a voice started.

Ah leave her at it. No need digging up bones yet.

Aye! There's plenty of time for bone digging before the Solstice.

"Before the Solstice? What's happening on the Solstice?" Gretchel asked, and was fully aware of a woman staring at her from across the next lane.

Ye can't be asking things like that. The devil's bride 'll be after ye!

"What is happening on the Solstice?" Gretchel persisted.

Silence. No more information was granted. "Wonderful," Gretchel muttered. She turned and made eye contact with the woman in the next lane. It was Troy's accountant. *Of course. Just wonderful!*

She loosened her panicked grip on the steering wheel, centered and focused on the road. She had to prove to Eli and her family that she was capable of taking care of herself. She also had to prove it to herself.

She pushed back the anxiety, and started the shopping frenzy: hardware store, farmers market, fabric store and then the dreaded everything-mart. Running into acquaintances was going to be a given at the last stop. Even so, she was going incognito. She'd dressed nondescript, or at least she thought, in a pair of snug jeans, a deep red quarter length turtleneck sweater, and old running shoes. It was casual yet presentable. Back in her days of numbness, she would have used her precious long red tresses as a curtain to hide behind while shopping, at parties or at her kid's sporting events. But now she didn't even want people to know she was in the vicinity. She wished she had a wig. She pulled her long red hair through a navy blue St. Louis Cardinals hat, and clipped it in a bun. She pulled the bill of the hat down low, just above her chiseled nose.

None of this helped much. It's hard to hide a six-foot redhead, much less a strikingly beautiful six-foot redhead. There were beautiful women in the world, and then there was Gretchel-beautiful. And even if she could have hidden her face, her Aphrodite-aura followed her like a seductive winter sunbeam down every aisle of the store.

She was stopped at every turn. The experience was brutal. Either it was a friend or customer of Troy's, or a friend of her brother's, or a parent from the high school. The comments and questions were all unoriginal: *How are you? Do you need anything? I'm always there for you. You've suffered so much. How is Zach? This must be very hard on the kids. We all miss Troy so much. He was such a good man. There will never be another. Is Ame okay? How did she wreck her car?* And the question that no one dare ask, but was dying to know, *Who is the new man in your life?*

Behind the pleasantries and questions, Gretchel projected that they were all remembering her childhood trauma, and just waiting to watch her go crazy again. Finally, an hour in, the voices began jabbering in her head and were a welcome relief from the onslaught of prying social leeches. Fed up with the nosiness of the Irvine community, Gretchel decided to let live and just talk back to the Scottish broads. Suddenly she found herself alone to finish her shopping uninterrupted.

Let the rumors of my newest insanity begin. I do not give a fuck, she lied to herself, and then continued answering the ancestor's teasing until she had left the store with plenty of stares, but without further hindrance.

She made a quick stop at a restaurant to pick up lunch. As she returned to her car, she heard her name being called. She instinctively turned and instantly grimaced.

"Gretchel!" Cody called again, trotting toward her. Cody Brown: Troy's best friend, Michelle Brown's husband and her former neighbor. *Goddamn it!*

"What next?" Gretchel whispered under her breath, and lobbed the take out into the car.

"How's Ame?" Cody breathlessly questioned.

"Fine. Fine, fine, fine. She's fine. She's got some therapy ahead of her, and her shoulder will probably never be the same, but she's fine." She'd answered this question at least sixty-three times already.

Cody let out a sigh of relief. "And how about you?" he asked looking her up and down. He noticed she'd gained weight. She looked radiant and healthy, if not fierce and utterly scrumptious. "I haven't seen you in months, Gretchel. You fell off the face of the earth."

"No. I did not. I had a chance to get away from the suburban life and I took it. What do you want?"

Cody flinched, and quickly rebounded. "It's not good for you to be alone at the cottage. It's not good for you to be alone period," he said appearing concerned, but fishing for information like everyone else.

"I'm not alone, and you know it," she said quietly.

"Yeah, I guess I do know," he replied. There was an awkward pause. There was always an awkward pause. "Are you getting ready for prom or Beltane?"

"Both," she said.

He nodded. "When is Zach coming home?"

"How dare you ask me about Zach?" she snarled. "You promised me you wouldn't let Bea take him, and now he's gone!"

"He left on his own free will, and how the hell was I supposed to know he was going?"

"He was living with you, Cody!" Gretchel cried. Tears glassed over her eyes. Thinking about Zach nearly tore her in two.

Cody cracked his knuckles, and scuffed his feet on the ground. "I can't win this argument."

"No you can't."

"Ben hasn't heard from him since the first week he left. He hasn't even been on any social media. Something's not right, Gretchel."

"Of course something's not right. His grandmother is crazy!"

Gretchel could tell Cody was considering the irony of her statement, and she had to force herself not to slap him.

"He needs to be back here, if not with you, with us."

"Not with you. You had your chance, which was what you wanted, and you failed." She poked him hard in the chest. "He will not go back with you, and your evil bitch of a wife."

Cody stared at the ground in shame. "Look, I'll drive up to Chicago myself if he's not home by summer."

Gretchel laughed contemptuously. "You do that Cody. Maybe you'll finally get your chance to be a hero."

"Don't start it with me, Gretchel."

"Oh fuck you, and fuck your fucking home-wrecking wife too."

∞

Gretchel zipped out of the strip mall, cursing Cody. Her ancestors started bickering all at once. She found herself driving downtown past the quaint little shops. The squawking in her head increased. It erupted as a migraine, and she found herself forced to stop until the pain eased. She put the car in park, and the obnoxious chatter abruptly stopped.

They're trying to tell me something.

Looking up she noticed she was in front of *Claire's Cauldron*. It was Ame's old place of employment. It had opened only the autumn before. Although Gretchel had never been in the store, she now felt herself being drawn to the front door.

Soft, soothing background music played, and the

store smelled of cherries and moss. There were shelves upon shelves of crystals and tarot cards, books and herbs, besoms and altar cloths. Gretchel smiled. It felt like home. Why had she never come here before? Ame had raved about the place.

"I thought you might be stopping by this week. I'm honored."

Gretchel spun around to see a stunning woman with long jet-black hair and pale white skin. Gretchel knew her. The woman was impeccably groomed. Her lips were full and pink. Her eyes were like aqua obsidian. Her beauty mesmerized Gretchel, and Claire was feeling much the same way about Gretchel.

"There are so very many things I would like to discuss with you, but I am bound to code and cannot," the woman or fairy or fairy-woman said.

Gretchel nodded in agreement. She couldn't quite put her finger on the deep knowing or connection that passed between them. "I know what you are, Claire. I remember you being at my house the night Eli returned to Irvine."

"I was indeed. Do you remember seeing me anywhere else? Recently?"

Gretchel tilted her head, considering. "No. Yes. Well, maybe, but it's very faint, like I saw you in the dream world."

Claire smiled and gently stepped closer to Gretchel. "Indeed. Can you remember the details of our visit?"

Gretchel picked up a piece of polished amethyst and clenched it in her fist. She closed her eyes and fervently tried to recollect. It was impossible. "I can't recall, but it feels *very* important. Please tell me."

"I cannot," Claire said. She took Gretchel's hands and held them together.

Gretchel immediately felt a sense of peace that she hadn't felt in a very long time. A vision formed in her mind. She saw a forest and a stream. She saw two lovers in a tight embrace. The scene changed and Gretchel saw Claire with the wings she secretly possessed. There were many fae. Gretchel saw a male with wings. She recognized him, and smiled at the validity of a hunch she'd had for years. Then she saw this male carving a box with a wand made from the ash tree.

Gretchel dropped the amethyst. She looked down at Claire. "I've seen that box before. I've seen it, and it terrifies me. Keep it the hell away from me!"

Claire was silent. Careful. Absolutely still.

"You can't discuss it at all?" Gretchel inquired.

"Not on this plane of existence."

"Keep it away from me!"

"You don't understand, Gretchel."

"I understand the evil it contains. Keep it away from me!" she cried and backed out the door as quickly as she could.

CHAPTER FOUR

Irvine, 2010s

Eli had just finished organizing hundreds of photos on his computer, when he heard the kitchen door slam. He jumped, startled. Apprehensively, he walked out of the bedroom clutching his laptop. Gretchel dumped bags onto the antique farm table. She marched back out, and slammed the door again. Eli had seen his mother and girlfriends in enough of these moods to know he'd better just shut up and help.

After all the bags were brought in, and everything was put away, Gretchel roughly tossed him his bag of lunch, walked into the studio and slammed the door. He could hear her talking to herself, arguing, and cursing.

"Just tell me what is going to happen on the Solstice!" she roared.

Silence.

"You bitches ain't seen crazy yet. You keep messing with me and I'll show you a bona fide lunatic!"

The hair stood on Eli's arms. He did not attempt to enter the studio. There was no source of water within the room, and *that* was a source of comfort to him. The one-sided conversation was still going strong when Ame returned from school. She entered the studio before Eli could warn her, and she came back out moments later.

"What's wrong with crazy lady now?" Ame asked.

Eli sighed. "She went into Irvine today to run errands–by herself."

"Great," she said with a dramatic eye-roll. "I'm sure I'll hear all about her experience tomorrow at school. It's a hoot having a schizophrenic for a mother."

That night, after dinner and lots of talking with his daughter, Eli shut off the living room light and shuffled to bed. Something was wrong with Gretchel, and he was going to have to press the issue to find out more. It was past midnight when Gretchel finally came into the bedroom. Eli heard her coming, and hid behind the door. She liked to be tickled. He planned to lighten her up with some midnight silliness.

It was pitch black. He grabbed her.

"Don't touch me! Don't touch me! Don't touch me!" She screamed, scraped at his arms and kicked him repeatedly.

Eli had to grab her with all his strength to calm her down, and to keep her from harming him.

"Gretchel it's me, damn it! It's Eli!" he called. He used an elbow to flip on the light.

She was shaking, holding herself, and staring at him through tears of terror. "Don't you ever do that to me again!" she scolded.

"I'm sorry. I'm so sorry. I was just playing. I'm so sorry, Gretchel." *Stupid, stupid, stupid, stupid!* he berated himself. *Who does such a thing to a woman with PTSD? Gods, I'm an idiot!* He was lucky she didn't have a full-blown psychotic episode.

She was still reeling. She undressed herself, and threw on a light blue camisole. Very carefully, she climbed into bed, trembling. She clutched the old redheaded rag doll to her chest, and pulled the covers up to her chin. She was still shaking like a leaf.

"Are you gonna be okay?" he asked timidly.

"I'm fine. You really frightened me. I didn't mean to overreact. It was just instinct."

"I'm so sorry."

"It's okay, Eli. Just drop it."

He nodded, and shamefully crawled into bed next to her. She flipped over and made to go to sleep. Eli couldn't handle the silence. When her shaking subsided, he decided to ask for some answers.

"Is there something you want to talk about?" he asked as gingerly as he could.

Gretchel let out an exasperating sigh. "I'm just busy this week. I'm stressed out, and I'm tired. I've had a headache most of the day. The voices have been ruthless, and your presence isn't helping much this time."

Eli considered this, and then he replied, "I understand that prom and Beltane are big deals. So is the prophecy? Is that what's bothering you?"

Gretchel groaned, wishing he would leave her alone.

"Maybe. Maybe it's lots of things. Maybe it's the people in my past that won't go away, maybe I miss my son, maybe I'm still freaked out that Graham Duncan is your father, maybe I feel like I'm being watched constantly, maybe I feel like my life is going to crumble apart at the drop of a hat. Maybe I really am insane. Did you know that Claire is a fairy? A fucking fairy lives in Irvine."

"Who's Claire?"

"Ame's former boss."

"Ohhhhh…" Eli said, and paused. He wasn't sure if what Gretchel was saying was believable or not, but based on his present life experience, he was in no position to argue. He chose to simply skip commenting on the subject altogether. "Gretchel, I've no doubt you have anguish," he said quietly. "And whenever you're ready, there is ample help and resources available."

Her face dropped and she nodded.

Eli decided not to push it further. Not yet. "You might be interested to know the deed to your country club home came in the mail today. My parents are going to stay there for a while if you don't mind."

"You bought my house?"

"I talked you into giving me the payment book, remember? But I don't make payments."

She stared at him. Shocked. "Please don't try to buy me, Eli. I've been there and done that. My days of hooking are over."

Eli felt like she'd shot him with an arrow. "How dare you?" he cracked. His face burned bright with anger.

"Oh I dare," Gretchel fumed. "And now your mother's here to stay. Goddamn it! I am totally excited to meet your father–he's Graham Duncan for fuck's sake–and once prom is over, I plan to spend a great deal of time with him." Eli's eyes narrowed. "Don't you look at me they way. It's your mother I can't stand to be around. She's hell-bent on revealing all of my secrets to the world. She looks at me like she knows things about me, things that I don't even know. She knows I'm a nutcase."

"Quit calling yourself a nutcase," he interjected.

"I feel like a nutcase!" she yelled and hopped out of bed. She indignantly paced the room. "I am a healing nutcase, but it takes time, and right now I'm fucking angry, and I want to be allowed to be fucking angry.

"I've told you some of my secrets; I've stretched my comfort zone, but under pressure. If I'm going to tell you or anyone else about the hell I've been through in my life, and about the demon that possesses me it's going to be on *my* terms. You know, Grand Mama was right, Marcus does coddle me and so do my mama and Teddy to an extent. I'm a big baby. *Baby Girl*. Of this I am aware. I've milked the sympathy teat dry, but none of my family has ever pressured me into speaking about things I can't yet speak about."

Maybe they should have, Eli thought.

"I know these secrets need to be told. I know that it's going to be the only way I heal, but let me do it my way. Please! Just let it come out naturally. I don't want to be pressured anymore, and I'm sick of all the attention focused on my possession or illness or whatever the hell it is. Everyone in this town knows I'm a nutcase. It's just the way it is. But I don't care about them. I care about you. I care about us. I want to wake up and know that I can love you and give you all of myself without having to put up the walls. Without thinking you're going to try and pry something loose that isn't ready to be loosened.

I'm tired of being a defensive bitch to you. You're my soft place to fall. My Hermes."

Eli was stunned. "I... I...," he stammered.

"You didn't realize you were doing it, I know, and I don't mean to be so passive aggressive. I don't mind being challenged, Eli. My whole life has been one big challenge that somehow I keep asking for, but your mother is going to push you to go too far with me. She's already planned something. I can sense it all over you. But you have to understand that I want the same thing you want. I want to be free of this burden, but I have to trust my own inner timing.

"I don't want to hurt your feelings, just back off the prophecy a little bit. I'm scared to death of myself right now. I am literally scared out of my mind, and you have no idea how much pain I'm in and how exposed and naked I feel without that amethyst around my neck, a knife cutting my skin or a drink in my hand!"

If the subject matter hadn't been so personal and heartbreaking, Eli might have given her speech a prized 'slow clap' just for delivering it with such gusto.

"I'm sorry, Gretchel," he said. He welcomed her back to bed, and kissed her freckled cheekbone. "I'm so sorry. I don't want to push you toward anything of that nature. I didn't know I was going too far."

"Yes you did," she snapped.

Nailed. "Yes. I guess I did. I'm sorry."

Gretchel softened. She was tired of fighting. She was just plain tired, and ready to sleep. "Apology accepted. Good night, Eli," she kissed his lips and then turned over.

Eli couldn't stop himself. "Gretchel, can I ask you

just one question without you freaking out? You are capable of *not* freaking out aren't you?"

He just has to keep prodding. She growled, and nodded her head wearily.

"Did you by any chance start your period?"

"Is it that obvious?"

CHAPTER FIVE
Irvine, 2010s

Despite the late night rant, Gretchel was up for her usual run with the dawn the next morning, and hadn't slowed down pace. Eli was giving her plenty of space, and by the time the elder witches of Snyder Farms, including Cindy, had gathered at the cottage by midmorning, Gretchel seemed to be behaving quite naturally if not normal–that is if she had a normal.

The four women were deeply involved in the beading of Ame and Holly's prom dresses. After attacking Gretchel's enormous Beltane to-do list, which included mowing the vast cottage property, Eli showered and crashed into the storybook chair. He quietly observed the women working, taking comfort in their own ways.

Ame's dress was a slinky number, ivory with olive and white glass beading, while Holly's was a bright blue, puffy thing with matching blue beading. Eli wasn't concerned with the detail of the dresses, but he was fascinated by the interaction of the women. Gretchel and

Ella, who clearly didn't connect on too many levels, were connecting during their sophisticated handiwork. Miss Poni would occasionally take a turn sewing a few beads, but her frail hands could not do many. Eli assumed it was more for her just to be involved.

Cindy, like always, paid close attention to her work, and Eli held her in the highest regard. She had given herself to this family. Good and bad, they were her life, and he knew that she wouldn't have it any other way.

Eli assisted Gretchel in the kitchen preparing a lunch of eggplant parmesan and salad for the group. He could tell she was feeling better after the scare the night before. The steam she'd let off certainly helped relieve her stress about going into Irvine. She would smile at him, and bump him with her hip. He would wink at her, and she would grin from ear to ear. It was the way it was supposed to be, or at least how he expected it might be. Innocent and playful, with a knowing that there was someone else on the face of the earth that understood your logic, and loved you anyway.

Eli had also slipped into Irvine to help his parents get settled. Diana's assistants had flown in the day before and had the house well furnished. Eli was very grateful that he wasn't the one taking care of his mother's detailed agenda; Gretchel's was currently more than he could handle.

A flatbed trailer held his as well as his father's custom motorcycles. He thought it might be fun to take a trip to Carbondale with Graham on the bikes once all was said and done. It would be nice to visit the House on Pringle; the house he had spent so much time in as a child with his father and grandmother, while his mother was traveling the world in search of Gretchel. The irony was just so mind-boggling when he thought how the circle had been closed at the very house where he waited for his mother to return home, year after year.

When Eli returned to the cottage, he walked into a room full of feminine laughter and bright smiles. Ame and Holly had returned from school, and now there were four generations of women delighting in their own creations. It was a joy to see them all open and happy, especially Gretchel. Ame had been right. This was not something Eli could buy her at any store. This was divine connection.

Eli snapped picture after picture of the holy gathering. The women essentially ignored him, and continued to laugh and carry on as Miss Poni told stories about the lighter side of farm life. All of the redheads and the one blonde were in stitches. He thought that Gretchel was a very lucky girl to have so much family, and he could see nothing but graciousness in her eyes. This was his Gretchel. The one he remembered. The sacred circle was healing her, as circles often do.

∞

There was fresh electricity in the air as twilight descended upon the cottage. Graham and Diana had come for dinner. Though they hadn't expected any obligatory hospitality, Gretchel insisted. She needed to come to terms with Graham being who Peter was, and she needed to do it in her own quiet way.

"What's happenin' Grandpa Graham? G-Square, G-

Dizzle my fizzle?" Ame asked with a smirk on her face and a hand on her hip, welcoming the wild man into her home.

"Oh, Gingerbread you've no idea how long I've waited to hear someone call me Grandpa, but G-Square will suffice," he cackled madly, and pulled her into a large embrace.

Graham turned to Gretchel. "And the last I saw of you, your head was bouncing off the floor. How's that noggin, Honeylove?"

Gretchel let him embrace her lightly. She couldn't handle more than that at the moment. She would go into overwhelm again.

And so an hour-long discussion about Graham Duncan's latest best-selling and controversial novel, *Pan's Rebirth,* commenced between Eli, Diana, Graham, Ame and Holly. Gretchel shyly listened and took it all in.

Is it him? It's really him! she determined.

She was a bundle of nerves having Graham in the house. She couldn't look him in the eye like she had when she thought he was just Peter, Eli's dad. He was way more than that now. It was like being in high school, and the boy you most crushed on was watching you relentlessly.

Ame and Holly were absolutely giddy with anticipation, and Eli had a feeling it was more for Beltane than prom. Ame was over the moon with excitement. Troy had banned Pagan related celebrations, rituals and tools from their home. Ame studied in secret, of course, but to celebrate a sabbat was something she hadn't expected to do until the freedom of college.

It wasn't the first time the celebration had been

banned, Gretchel told the group, during a home-cooked meal of pork loin, mashed sweet potatoes and leftover salad from lunch. Gretchel reminded them of Colin Ferguson, Miss Poni's ruthless father.

"I'm grateful that Grand Mama was able to keep these precious traditions alive even though she had to keep them secret as a child. Beltane has always been particularly special to this family because it's Mama's birthday."

Gretchel explained to the group, but mostly to Ame, that Beltane was a fertility festival most often celebrated on May 1st. It was a time to celebrate the end of winter and welcome the abundance and warm days of spring and summer. It was a time to offer gratitude, and to ask for continued growth of their crops. There was the May Pole, the bon fire, dancing, and a bit of sexual indulgence, but she thought it best to leave that part out in front of the girls. She explained that it was a lot like Samhain, in that the veil separating the worlds was thinner than normal. It was a perfect time to catch a glimpse of the fairies.

Gretchel was impressed that she felt confident enough to share her knowledge in front of Graham Duncan. That was until he looked at her dead in the eye and asked, "Do you believe in fairies, Kittycat?"

She nearly choked. She couldn't lie to Graham Duncan. "Yes I do."

He smiled. "I do too. I have a friend who is a fairy, she…"

"Enough of your nonsense, Graham," Diana interrupted. She'd been watching Holly. The girl's eyes were fearful as she listened closely to discussion of the fae. Holly finally noticed Diana staring at her, and she quickly looked down at her food.

"In any case," Graham continued, "your description of Beltane was lovely. We've been to the Edinburgh Fire Festival in Scotland many times, and it's always a delectable treat. A Green Man and the May Queen always preside over the festivities."

"Mama is always our May Queen, and my father…" Gretchel hesitated, "…my dad was always our Green Man." Eli watched Gretchel, as she quickly backed up from the table and took her plate to the kitchen, her eyes lost in her frame of mind.

"I don't even want to go to prom anymore," Ame said under her breath. "I really don't. I feel like I need to be *here*."

"Whit's fur ye'll no go by ye," Holly whispered.

"What did you say?" Diana asked, attempting nonchalance.

"Nothing," Holly murmured.

Interesting, Diana thought. *This girl knows something.*

"Do we have to go to prom, Mom?" Ame whined.

Gretchel returned from the kitchen and gave Ame *the look*. "Just kidding," Ame winched. "Tell the little voices in your head that I retreat." She waved her napkin in surrender, and Holly snickered at her cousin's antics.

"Who's your date, Ame?" Diana asked. Gretchel and Eli both wondered as well. Peyton's name hadn't been mentioned all week.

Ame shifted in her seat. "I'm going with my old boyfriend Peyton, but he doesn't really want to go. Says he's too old for high school stuff, but he's gonna take me anyway. You see he's currently on the shit list," she said, and then glared at her mother.

"That's not a great way to start a relationship young lady. It sounds very manipulative," Diana remarked.

"Do you know a lot about manipulation, Granny Stewart?" Ame quipped.

Eli and Gretchel both looked at each other shocked. Graham quickly changed the subject to a new car. Ame was thinking perhaps a Corvette this time. Gretchel was thinking perhaps not.

It was past eight when Diana asked Ame and Holly to take her around town. She insisted Eli go too, and he understood her motives. Ame hadn't been wrong: manipulation *was* Diana's calling.

∞

Graham helped Gretchel clean up the kitchen. He chose a rare Pink Floyd album, *Obscured By Clouds*, to put on the record player, and quietly hummed to himself.

"Where did you find that album, Honeylove?" he called to Gretchel.

She had no clue where it came from. "Most of those records are my brother's." Gretchel was strangely uncomfortable–meaning she was completely comfortable, but felt that in the presence of her hero she was turning into a melted stick of butter, a puddle of goo, a single-celled blob of incoherence and indecision.

"Well, what do you want to do," she asked, after the dishwasher was started, and the last counter was finally wiped clean. She finally looked up at the man, and knew she'd just asked the wrong question.

There was a dangerous silence.

"I hear you enjoy dancing," he finally said.

She shook her head vehemently. "Not anymore."

Graham had an irresistible *come-hither* look on his face as he stepped toward her. He took the dishtowel out of her hand, and, never releasing his hold on it or her, tossed it onto the counter. Then he swung her around, and danced her slowly and silently around the kitchen. He never even considered asking first. It didn't matter. She was swooning in his strong arms after the first spin.

Graham Duncan. This is Graham Duncan, the realization finally sunk in.

His face was inches from hers and she thought for sure he was going to kiss her, when he whispered in her ear, "I think I'd like to see Epona."

Gretchel let out an ambivalent sigh of relief. *Thank Goddess.*

CHAPTER SIX

Irvine, 2010s

Suzy-Q ran amok as Graham casually played with her on the way to the Wicked Garden. It was bizarre how quickly the dog had taken to Graham, and with such exuberance. Their energy radiated mutual acceptance. Even Epona could feel the warmth, as she trotted up to meet the man, this, despite Gretchel being in such close proximity.

"You're splendiferous, an absolute treasure," Graham told the mare, stroking her mane. The horse seemed to be enjoying his caress, and Gretchel was suddenly quite jealous.

"When I was a kid I had a black mare named Pixie. She died suddenly. Horses haven't liked me since," she said keeping her distance. "And *I* only like white or painted horses now anyway."

Graham gave her a funny glance. *What is she insinuating?*

"So what do you have against Epona?" he asked. "You're not an equine racist are you?"

"Well look at her. She's black as night. She reminds me of the night mare, who has haunted my dreams since I was a child," Gretchel laughed incredulously, as her narcissistic archetype came shining through. She acted as if Graham should already know this basic fact about her.

Graham's face fell. *Oh sweet dumpling, you can't be serious. Please tell me it's a joke*, he thought. But it was no joke. She *was* serious. He cataloged the information, and continued to stroke the horse. "She has a very calm temperament, but I bet she's a bit feisty when provoked, not unlike the human who cares for her."

Gretchel kicked at the earth. "Yep. She can get a little pissy when a crazy broad has plans to fire a shotgun in her direction," Gretchel stated coldly. She turned away from the horse and stood at the edge of the Wicked Garden staring at the burnt up pickup truck. She immediately clutched her abdomen.

Graham was instantly at her side. "Enter?"

"Hell no. This place is haunted, Graham. It's evil and sinister, and it's forbidden."

"I beckon the forbidden. And how many times have you been in the Wicked Garden in the past six months?"

Gretchel hesitated. "A few."

"Well Kittycat, I'm not big on rules, and ghosts don't scare me. Stay if you want, but I was under the impression that you walked your own path."

Gretchel refused to be outwitted. She stepped in time with the crazy-haired fellow, and they entered the Wicked Garden together. In an act of extreme bravery she reached her hand out, and touched the side of the truck. It was the first time she had touched it in a calm mental state. The truck's vibe was calm as well, and Gretchel was surprised by that revelation. *That'll fool him*, she thought.

Graham cleared his throat, and then spoke. "I must warn you ahead of time that I've been asked to take any clues you give me about your past back to Admiral Diana at command central."

"My psychic abilities, even as out of practice as they may be, have already alerted me of your intentions. Take what you want Mr. Duncan, but I'll warn *you* ahead of time that the demon inside me, unlike myself, is very careful about locking doors behind her."

Her moxie is going to be the death of me, and I shall die a blessed and happy man, Graham smiled.

Suzy-Q began digging in front of the old truck. Neither paid her much mind, Graham was too busy delighting in Gretchel's sass, and Gretchel was too busy thinking of ways to control it. Suddenly, Epona shook herself out briskly, and a tingle ran through both Gretchel and Graham.

They turned to each other.

"Did you feel that?" Gretchel whispered. Graham shook his head. It was a very pleasant rush. "Weird things always happen in the Wicked Garden."

Graham turned back to the horse. *What do you know my equine friend?* he thought. *What secrets are you attempting to share?* Epona nudged his shoulder, but Graham was still clueless.

He turned back to Gretchel. "It's the eve of Beltane, Honeylove. Let's build a fire."

Gretchel didn't move.

"We used to have a big bon fire down here every

year when I was a kid. That particular part of the tradition stopped after the accident," she said and didn't look, but pointed a sideways thumb toward the truck. "The tradition didn't begin again until Troy banned me from attending. Marcus and Cindy are burning one up at his house as we speak with their friends. I'm sure the girls will be up there later. You can go if you'd like. I'm sure it's much more exciting than this."

"A man doesn't need constant excitement. I appreciate calmness just as much. I'm stoked right where I am, but tell me, why aren't *you* there?" Graham asked.

"I'm a recovering alcoholic. Their friends are probably drinking, and I'd rather not be around that right now. With the necklace gone, I'm not sure I could handle the drunken festivities or my impulses. I couldn't handle the huge blaze of any fire after the accident, and I'm not sure if I can handle it tomorrow either. Did you know my husband was a firefighter at one time? Isn't that ironic?"

"Coincidental maybe, but I doubt it was an accident," he smiled. "The past and the future are just pages in the scrapbook of our imagination. Perhaps you could handle a small fire now–in the present moment, perfectly sober."

He was pushing her, but in her mind, *his* pushing was okay. In her mind, Graham Duncan doing anything was okay. "Maybe a small one," she grinned coyly. "I *am* a little chilly."

They quickly gathered kindling from a patch of woods beyond the garden. Soon, a small fire was crackling. Graham, with some effort, was able to pull the tailgate down on the all but destroyed truck, and they both sat lotus style on the Texas bench.

"May Cernunnos return this once fertile and now wicked ground back to its sanctity," Graham said in a hushed tone as he blessed the Wicked Garden, and broke their long silence.

Gretchel chuckled, and Graham looked at her waiting to be filled in. "My best friend, Teddy, used to call me Fertile Myrtle."

"You only have two children," he remarked.

"I've had four pregnancies," she said, and then grimaced. *Why do I keep telling these Duncan men secrets I don't wish them to know?*

Graham saw the unease, and decided to move in another direction.

"I noticed you didn't mention anything earlier about Beltane being a day of sexual freedom, when infidelities are overlooked and even encouraged," he teased. "What gives?"

Gretchel tensed. She tried to control her rage. She certainly didn't want him to see this side of her, but the emotion came charging out of her without permission.

"My husband and my father are dead, Graham. I don't need to set aside a specific day to experience sexual freedom. There's no overlooking needed anymore. I have all the sexual freedom I want without the fear that I'll be beat to death if I should happen to exercise that freedom. I've learned that sexual freedom doesn't give you the right to hurt somebody else with your indecencies. I've done my share of bending the rules, and all it gave me in return was a web of lies that I still have to contend with to this day.

"I don't need a ring on my finger or to be

handfasted with Eli to know that he is my one and only. I will never betray him, and it has nothing to do with sexual or personal freedom. It has to do with loving that person selflessly and with complete trust. He is the one. He has always been the one."

Graham's eyes were wide. *This woman isn't a firecracker,* he thought.... *oh no... this ginger pie is a lit stick of dynamite.* "Has menses come to visit you, Honeylove?" he asked.

"Is it that freaking obvious? Can't a woman rage just because she needs to fucking rage? Men do it all the time. Where is the goddamn code of conduct? Where is the fucking feminine rulebook? I want possession of it, so I can burn the motherfucker to ashes!"

It took all of Graham's grace not to laugh with love. He inhaled the cold April air through his nostrils and grinned. "Honeylove, it is a fact that many women rage during their menses. It was not meant to be an insult, just an observation. I don't feel the need to continue defending myself. Rightful rage is nothing to be ashamed of. Go ahead and work yourself into a tizzy. It seems as though there is a lot more where that came from, and you don't scare me anyway."

His words disempowered her raging thoughts. She was humbled, and spoke softer, "I haven't had a period in three years. It was never normal after the accident, but I would always eventually cycle."

She grimaced again. *Why in the hell are we talking about my period anyway?* she wondered. She felt mortified all at once. She wanted to talk books instead, and spirituality, and wild campy fun. This was an abomination!

Graham took her hand, and kissed it. "What happened three years ago to make the cycle up and leave?" She looked down at the earth in shame. *He's pushing me too far.* "Kittycat, your silence doesn't impress me."

"Well what does impress you Mr. Duncan?"

"Courage." He smiled and tickled her hand with his middle finger.

She uncrossed her long legs and let her boots kick at the dirt for a long time before she spoke. She couldn't believe he was going to get to her. *How is he doing this?*

"Okay. I was on my period then actually. I was sleeping soundly that night. I woke up in complete darkness when a piece of duct tape was abruptly slapped over my mouth. I thought somebody had broken into the house. No. It was my husband drunk after golf league. He gripped my hands, put them behind my back and wrapped them also with duct tape."

Gretchel paused. Graham held her hand tighter. She kicked at the dirt harder.

"Troy, my husband of many years, proceeded to violently rape me. Troy was traditional, but not old-fashioned. He was creatively brutal with his assault."

Gretchel scanned the Wicked Garden until she spotted *Exhibit A* stuck in the weeds. She hopped off the tailgate to retrieve a sorry-looking pitching wedge. She stood in front of Graham, and ever so gently swung the club, perfectly chipping a stone into the fire.

"Nice shot," Graham said tenderly. "Is that the club you used earlier this month to beat the demon out of this truck? The night Eli showed up?"

"Well there's that," she chuckled lightly. She

chipped another stone directly into the flames, and then evaluated the damage the club had sustained from the truck beating. "But this was also the instrument Troy used for his torture. He raped me with this club. And after he raped me, he used it to beat me. This club right here," she pointed. Tears began to pour down her face. "It is a wonder I'm alive. I've escaped death more than once. Though some days I wonder how and I wonder why."

Graham held his breath. He knew he was dealing with an unpredictable woman, and he knew the danger that lingered.

As if on cue, she slammed the side of the truck with the club. Then she slammed it over and over and over again.

The impact rattled the truck and Graham to their core. The anger in the vibration was deep, and probably ancient.

She finally stopped, and flung the club back into the weeds with a mighty toss. She bent over, and took a moment to catch her breath, then wiped the tears from her face, and hopped back onto the tailgate.

Graham sat silent. It was many moments before Gretchel could speak again.

"After he was done torturing me he finally just passed out. I crawled my way to Ame's room. She released the bondages and called Troy's best friend, our neighbor across the street. They took me to the emergency room where Teddy met us. I insisted Cody, Troy's friend, leave. I didn't want him any more involved than he already was, and I didn't want his miserable cunt of a wife to find out. I made him swear to secrecy, though I know he wanted to murder Troy with his bare hands. I shouldn't have burdened him like that, but he was the closest person I could trust and Ame didn't have a driver's license yet.

"I was in the hospital for a few days. The bloody bedding had been replaced, and carpet had been steam-cleaned before I returned home. Troy acted as if nothing ever happened. He literally never spoke of the assault. He told everyone, including my son Zach, that I was having female troubles, but I know Zach knew his father had really banged me up good that time.

"Cody begged me to leave. Teddy begged me to leave. Neither would tell my brother Marcus or my family what really happened, though they all knew it was something terrible. Grand Mama even renovated the cottage, thinking it would sway me into leaving, but of course it didn't. I never pressed charges. I was born with a strange guilt that I cannot for the life of me let go of. There was a part of me that believes I deserved the rape."

"Honeylove, you have no idea how completely wrong that thought process truly is. Do you relish being a victim? Have you always craved punishment?" Graham intervened.

"Not always," she said.

"When did you start?"

"Nice try, but you're going too far, Mr. Duncan. Back to my story, I never left Troy. I never made it out the front door. When that club was tearing me I felt like I was going to die; I wished for it. I fought as hard as I could, and then I went into some sort of submissive trance. It must have been my body's way of surviving. I remembered reacting that way before. It wasn't the first time I'd been raped, but not by Troy. That's another story in and of itself, and one that can never, ever, *ever* be told. Not to you, not to my family, not to Eli, not to a psychiatrist, not to anyone, so please don't even try. It's in the vault, and it will stay there until I die."

But you're just itching to tell someone, aren't you Kittycat, Graham thought.

"Anyway, I completely lost myself after the club attack. I was a body without a spirit until I took off the amethyst necklace, and this is the first menstrual cycle I've had since then."

Graham was very careful. He roughly considered all the information, and spoke. "Why *did* you stay, Honeylove? What possessed you to stay with such a violent man? Why do women do this?"

"It's not that easy to just walk away when you don't know any better, and are too scared to hope."

Graham pulled her close to him. "Not easy, but possible. You always had a choice." Gretchel looked at him, and just as she prepared to argue, he interjected. "Thank you for telling me your story. I am thoroughly impressed with the courage you conjured to communicate, and it came out so easily. Why do you suppose that is?" he asked.

"Believe me I wish I knew, so I could find a way to stop sharing my secrets."

"You do know, Gretchel."

She released herself from his embrace, and peeked up at his aquamarine eyes that twinkled in the firelight. They were hypnotizing. She unconsciously moved a curl away from his forehead so she could see them better.

"I trust you," she whispered. "I don't know you, I'm totally intimidated by who you are, and I don't think I'll ever get over that, but for some reason I trust you. I trust you more than Eli. I trust you with everything that I am. I trust you with my life, and I think I always have."

All the fan letters that eventually made their way to his home, all the websites designed in his name, all the cults that traveled the country in search of him, and not one of them could have given the great Graham Duncan this kind of compliment, this praise that made his heart thump the sweetest rhythm. It wasn't an ego-driven song, but one that carried much responsibility. Responsibility he was born to uphold.

"The Beltane fire is purifying you as it was meant to do," he finally said, breaking the sacred silence.

Graham smiled his beautiful smile, and for a moment Gretchel saw a hint of Ame in his face. She chuckled at the resemblance, and watched as Graham pulled a hitter box out of his blazer pocket. He loaded the rod, and handed it to her.

"I haven't smoked pot in a very long time," she said. "It always seemed rather like a childish indulgence."

Graham chuckled. "It's not your drug of choice, I see."

"I always preferred a good Scotch," she said, and a lump caught in her throat.

"Not to worry, but it might help with the cramping," he smiled. She looked down and noticed she was holding her abdomen.

"It's not because of my cycle," Gretchel spat. "It's phantom pain. I usually get it when I'm around this blasted truck and the Wicked Garden." She took the hitter, and his lighter and fired it up. She blew the smoke out immediately, and coughed. "This is crazy, and so am I," she said, trying to catch her breath.

"Crazy is such a musty word. It bores me."

Gretchel looked at him with furrowed brows, which Graham ignored. He took the hitter back, and smoked what was left. He then sat back, and Gretchel prepared herself for one of his famous rants. She'd been looking forward to this, though she had no idea how he could possibly convince her she was sane.

"You're are an absolutely, stunningly beautiful woman whose spirit is being tormented by memories, complexes and the shadow side of an archetype. Is it a haunting too? It seems that way. I can see you're trying to reclaim your spirit as your own. You must have wanted to, you must have had a desire to, or else you never would have taken off the amethyst. You heard a true voice from inside you, the wild feminine. She knew it was time, and you listened. Your timing is impeccable.

"You're doing much soul work. You're bringing yourself close to nature, which I can tell fills you up and connects you with Self. You're reestablishing your creative life. You're surrounding yourself with people who love and inspire you, instead of the mindless leeches whose mediocrity sucked from you like vampires at a blood bank yard sale. You're mothering your child with grace and tenacity. You're gazing into your lover's eyes and seeing truth. All this is good, but there are still many open wounds that need healing. They are old, ancient wounds, and while you may have physical scars to prove that they happened, on the inside those wounds haven't healed either. You can admit now that they're there–that you no longer deny–but you aren't doing what it takes to heal them completely. You aren't taking complete responsibility for the mending. The scars have served their bigger purpose, Kittycat. I think you and I both know it's time to let them heal over already, the way nature intended."

CHAPTER SEVEN

Irvine, 2010s

Gretchel's mouth hung open in conspicuous bewilderment. It was several minutes before she was able to absorb humility and speak. "You have me pegged pretty good, Mr. Duncan," she finally whispered and bumped his shoulder. He reloaded the hitter, and passed it back to her.

"Tell me love, do you consider yourself a witch?"

Gretchel looked at him sideways. *Where is he going now?* she wondered.

"I don't adhere to labels very well. They are too sticky and hard to peel off once they've been applied. I change my mind about things constantly, but if you define a witch as someone who sees the energy and meaning of life in everything, then by gods yes, I am a witch. If you define a witch as someone who knows she is part of the cycle of life and not superior to it, then yes, I am a witch. Do I use my natural intuition, occasionally cast spells, and honor nature? Yes sir, I do. Do I have psychic and sensitive gifts? I do, albeit rusty. But, I'm careful with words, Graham. You said it yourself in *Pan's Rebirth*: words have power and an energy all their own. Words give meaning and value, but they also stigmatize. It all depends on perspective and reception."

Graham hopped off the tailgate and added more sticks to the fire. "Are you *afraid* to call yourself a witch?"

"Of course not. Everyone in this town knows I'm a witch. I simply couldn't practice my faith openly for seventeen years of my life. I am indeed a witch. However, I feel it's my right as a human being to change my mind at any given time, and allow others to do the same. Now if what I believe in could be defined, I would say it is Pantheism. I can identify and tolerate every god and goddess I've ever learned about, even the ones I've never mentioned or uttered. I see them as part of the collective consciousness. They are patterns of source energy. They are part of our universe, and I am a part of our universe. I'm living out a life of premeditated patterns, yet I have the free will to decide how I'm going to live them out. I get this; this is my human right. I get to stand in any circumstance wherever the path has taken me, and I get to make a choice."

Graham hopped back on the tailgate, and settled himself for more of Gretchel's glazy-eyed rhetoric.

"I can learn from every religion, every philosophy, every deity and every being. They all offer wisdom. I take what I need to sustain myself, and move on. Many times I come back around and revisit the same idea, perhaps because I wasn't ready for it the first time. I don't think spirituality is meant to be stagnant. It is meant to free us from the moment, which has become the past. Religion and spirituality are meant to keep us in the moment, and if that moment feels bad or offers us no useful growth, and many times it doesn't, then that is when I exercise the right to change my mind. It is not about being fickle or doing what suits me. It is doing what suits my soul and my spirit. It is about expansion and growth and freedom."

"I am a hereditary witch, and unashamed. Yes I do pray to the Goddess and the Horned God more than any other. It was how I was raised... yes, but I have the ability to look beyond the figurehead, beyond this label of what they should be, and I just see them as the force, the energy, and it's the same force as all the rest, just in a different guise or form. The bottom line is that energy is what makes the world go 'round, and that energy is what I am. Call me a witch, a bitch or whatever you like. It really doesn't matter to me."

Graham was beaming. *Eli is a lucky man, a very lucky man, indeed.*

"It's been a while since you've had the courage to put to words how you feel, and you weren't even sure you still had it in you. You're torn because you want so badly to live your life the way you just explained, but the demon is holding you back," he said, and roared on the tailgate.

Oh! How does he know these things? "You're right again, Mr. Duncan. I'm waking up from a cold, cruel slumber, and it feels rather nice at times. My ideas have evolved, but I've always been just a tad abnormal in my views. My brother was very interested in metaphysics before he chose to take over the farm. Devon, his best friend in college, majored in sociology. You should have heard the conversations I listened to as a child. I couldn't help but be enthralled by the mysteries."

"I'd love to talk to Marcus in depth," Graham said.

"I'm sure the feeling's mutual. He's been reading your work long before me. Devon is the one who gave me your first book. I was only thirteen."

Graham smiled proudly. He couldn't even imagine a thirteen-year-old making sense of the risible prose that came from his mind.

"You were raised with Celtic tradition, married a Christian man who didn't behave very Christ-like, and you consider yourself a child of the Tao. I do say you get around. We could have a lot of fun together you and I," he teased. "I'm thinking a cave in the mountains. We could dance naked around the clock." She attempted to cover her chagrin with laughter. "Tell me, Honeylove, do you follow the natural cycles that you claim to be a part of?"

Gretchel hesitated, and then blew out more smoke. "I try. I have trouble with cycles. Chaos, obsession and addiction seem to be my way."

Graham chuckled at her flippantness. "The natural cycle is a give and take that the universe not only expects, but continues to dish out whether you're focused on what you want or not."

Gretchel shook her head in agreement. "I think I may have gotten hung up within that cycle. It feels like a part is broken, and I can't make the wheel spin again. But I do understand the connection and the gratitude. I believe in the magic of the cycle. I've always believed in the magic," she said.

"Magic may be the only honorable thing to believe

in," Graham stated. "And that of course is a paradox in itself. Faith makes us human. Faith that the sun will rise in the morning. Faith that the cosmos will continue to be, whether we are able to experience it as fully conscious humans or as rocks. What has the world up in arms is their attachment to belief. Belief and labels stifle original thought and pigeonhole a person into a set of values they may not necessarily care to follow the next day or even the next minute, as you said. Ideas on the other hand are less tangible, but closer to the freedom of truth. When a person has an idea, it's just that, an idea. You're not chained to it, it's not a burden, it's just a thought, and a thought can move mountains, depending on how the thought makes you feel. It's all about perception and the feeling of that perception. The remarkable thing about a thought is that...."

"....a thought can change."

Graham slapped his knee. "Exactly. So tell me more of your thoughts, Honeylove? What other kind of magic do you brew under that long crimson crown?"

Gretchel handed back the hitter, and began feeling the influence of the weed.

"Well I think that the world is a very beautiful place. I think everything we need to survive has already been given to us. The proof is that we are breathing. I think there is a place for modern technology, for material goods and consumerism, but I think we've gone too far too quickly. In general, society doesn't know when to say enough is enough. That is the problem with much of humanity is it not? We either go too far or we don't go far enough. I am an addict and struggle to know when enough is enough, or even when I don't have enough of what I really need.

"I think life is about experiencing and learning from individual moments. I think these moments can turn into an extraordinary flow.... *if*.... you can find a healthy harmony. Harmony is key. Riding the wave is euphoria to me. I don't mind making mistakes as long as I learn something from them. I've always been that way. I've always craved experience, which may be my best and worst attribute."

She paused and picked at a rusted spot on the old truck.

"I think the soul is an emotional container, and the spirit, when working properly, is in motion and responsible for filling up the soul container. They work together seamlessly in a healthy functioning being. You're right that I am a child of the Tao. It is no different than the witch's path. I think there is feminine energy and I think there is masculine energy, which is how I've attempted to raise my children, though I wasn't able to do it openly or with much ardor as I would have liked. I think life is about finding the balance between them, and truly feeling the ride along the way, no matter what way it takes you. I feel both of those energies. Sometimes it's light and free, other times it's very dark and dense. I think the one is made up of the two, and the two cannot survive without one another. In a spiritually healthy being they balance each other. I think to be too one-sided is dangerous. Too much rapture, though quite lovely and necessary, can actually damage the soul. But too much darkness can be even worse, even deadly. I've been an ice queen and a hot emotional mess. I have no balance, but that doesn't mean I don't believe in it.

"Harmony. I think life's not so much about thinking and doing as it as about *feeling* what you're thinking and doing. I've had two phases in my life when I couldn't feel much at all. Once when I was a teenager, which was probably the worst part of my life, and then after I put on the amethyst necklace. When Eli put it around my neck it saved me, that much I know is true, but I had to sacrifice my feelings to accept the salvation. It started out slow, and as the years progressed I just became numb. I was the walking dead. I was a ghost of a being. There was very little of my wild spirit left when I took off that necklace, but what was left, was just enough.

"Was it worth it for me to accept that amethyst, that magic if you will? To protect my daughter, of course, and I am grateful to Eli, Diana and Fate, but sometimes I wonder if maybe I should have gone through the active alcoholism, the rise and fall of the addiction. Maybe I should have taken the necklace off many years ago. The demon inside me didn't care either way. Numb and alcoholism seems to be congruent in my perception. Sometimes I wonder if maybe I was robbed of something very important; a lesson about human courage and persevering through struggle. It is what I am backtracking and trying to learn now. I don't crave the drink as much as I crave the numbness. It hurts to feel.

"One thing I do know for sure is that I *am* feeling again, but it's not a harmonious feeling. I know I come off as a polar bear that isn't sure which igloo she needs to topple. I can see this clearly, but I need more time. I spent seventeen years trapped in fuzzy country club hell. I spent seventeen years missing out on the emotional gratification of being a mother. Yes, I was there for my children, I loved them, and I was able to show it the best I could, but it wasn't the true me. There was no Tao.

"Ame's getting to know *this me* now, and it's not easy for her. That brings my thoughts to Zach, who I feel like I've cheated out of everything. He's a good boy, Graham, but he's lived a lie just like Ame. He had an awful role model fathering him and a mother who wasn't capable of giving him the maternal guidance he needed. I miss him. I want him back. I think about him a lot, but I know he has to work through his own grief concerning his dad. I won't let him turn out like me. And how I got from the universal source to my son I'll never know.... I think I'm stoned."

Graham's smile was as broad as the barn beside him.

"That was a beautiful, honest, thought-provoking rant my dear. You've given me a run for my money. Do go on. I get tired of the sound of my own vox box, and I could listen to your fantastic pontifications all night long," he smiled.

"Anything else you want to know while I'm full of sweet leaf?" Gretchel asked.

There were many things Graham wanted to know, but one important thing that would make this whole night a success for his wife. "Where's the box Gretchel?"

Her face morphed from a goofy smile to an angry snarl, and before she could snap, Suzy-Q began barking madly.

"Hush it dog!" she hollered, and jumped up to charge the hound. The barking continued, and Epona pranced in place. Both animals stood at the front of the truck. "Suzy-Q, knock it off!" Gretchel screeched.

The dog finally listened and held in its noise. She sat panting nervously, while Epona paced the fencerow.

Gretchel walked back to Graham, and sharply pointed at his face. "That box is none of your business, Graham Duncan!"

"What's inside it, Gretchel?" Graham persisted, slightly stern in his reproach.

"I don't know where it is, and I don't know what's inside. I want nothing to do with it. Does Diana know about the box?" Gretchel demanded.

"She does."

"Is it in the prophecy?"

"It is."

"When do I get to see the whole prophecy?"

"When you tell Diana your story."

"You tell her she can go to hell."

"Kittycat, Satan wants nothing to do with her."

"Figures."

They both snickered, and Graham knew the conversation about the box had officially ended. They were both strangely thankful.

Gretchel looked at him thoughtfully. "You remind me of the Green Man."

"How so, Kittycat?"

"You're an eternal child that follows the cycles. You wrote in *The Shaman's Slinky* about living a fully conscious life when you're awake, then dying when you go to sleep, allowing the dream world and your psyche to guide you, and then being reborn in the morning to create a new reality all over again. You're constantly allowing the cycle of life, death and rebirth to guide you.

How do you do that?"

Graham was very careful with his answer. This was a delicate woman, but a woman who needed to hear truth. His words were deliberate and honest. "I'm not afraid to live, I let die what needs to die, and I *always* welcome growth with open arms. I can tell you're not afraid to live Gretchel, but perhaps you could use a little assistance with the rest."

"Perhaps," she whispered.

"Gretchel, Sweetness, Kittycat, Cupcake, Honeylove, Turtledove... tell me what you want in this very moment."

"I don't know. I want my family to be happy."

"Too vague and oh so cliché! After that rant you just gifted me with? Come on! Listen to your body; listen to your soul. What is it that you *really* fucking want?"

She squinted and stared into the fire. "I have the munchies. I want something to eat, but not leftovers. I need dessert, maybe a popsicle. I just want something sweet to suck on."

Oh great googly, moogly! Graham thought.

CHAPTER EIGHT

Irvine, 2010s

It was late when Eli and Diana walked into the kitchen of the cottage.

Graham and Gretchel sat in the lotus position on the farm table facing each other, and laughing hysterically. The six-foot redhead was was mischievously eating a spoonful of green frosting. She wore a white camisole, old jeans and was, of course, barefoot. It was a vision of Aphrodite gone bohemian, and Eli felt his face flame with jealousy.

Graham sat barefoot and bare-chested, laughing as if Gretchel had just told the funniest joke ever written, which might have been true, considering her jesting nature. Even so, Eli was disgusted and hurt by the sight.

He walked straight up to the table and took Gretchel's hand. He launched the spoon full of frosting toward into the kitchen and it landed with a clank and thud. "Come on, Baby Girl. It's time for bed. You have a big day tomorrow."

Diana rolled her eyes. *They treat this woman like a*

precious doll. And speaking of dolls, she wondered if she could catch a glimpse of the rag doll of which Eli spoke.

"But I'm not done decorating the Green Man!" she protested with a whiney southern drawl.

Diana rolled her eyes *and* her head. She had to force herself to stay quiet.

Eli's head flipped toward his father. "You got her stoned; what a classy date."

Diana gave Graham a disapproving glare, and then looked to Gretchel and let loose. "Aren't you an alcoholic?"

"Mother!" Eli shouted.

Gretchel ignored Diana, and instead snapped at Eli. "And *you've* gotten stoned with Ame."

Diana huffed again, put her hands on her hips, and redirected her glare to Eli.

"Touché. Green Man, get the hell out of here and quit causing trouble," Eli stated contemptuously.

Graham knelt in and whispered into Gretchel's ear. "Until next time, my sweet ginger biscuit."

"Enough, *Peter*! Let's go," Diana called.

"You've forgotten my name again."

"Move it Graham!" Diana snapped, slapping her clutch on the table.

"If you insist, dear. Keep forgetting I have a whole new set of neighbors to break in. Just think of the possibilities in that docile country club setting." Graham rubbed his hands together in gleeful anticipation.

"That subdivision will never be the same," Gretchel giggled just as Eli picked her up and threw her over his shoulder. "Oh! And Graham, if you see an obnoxiously plastic blonde driving dealer plates, tell her Gretchel said 'fuck off and die'!"

Interesting, Diana thought. *Very interesting.*

∞

Diana marched through Gretchel's old home near the country club, picking up Graham's clothes along the way to the bedroom suite.

"Did you get anything out of the she-devil, Green Man?" she asked just as Graham stepped out of the shower.

"Diana, what do you have against Gretchel? Is her personality too strong for you? Do you feel threatened or does she turn you on too?"

Diana's face narrowed. "Of course I don't feel threatened! That giant, redheaded vixen doesn't intimidate me. But she does need a decent attitude adjustment, and to grow the hell up."

"I agree that she's running behind in the emotional growth department. I think she's emotionally stuck at about thirteen or fourteen-years-old. That often happens to children who suffer trauma or abuse. But I think she'll be one of those rare people who doesn't transform, but transcends. I've been waiting a long time to meet somebody with that capability. She's one of a kind, Diana. She and Eli are the perfect pair. They compliment each other so beautifully it's almost as if they were meant to be together."

"Then stop flirting with her, and let your son be happy. Isn't that what you keep reminding me? *Let him be happy. Let him be happy. Leave them alone.* And stop reminding me that she belongs with him. Of all the women in the world, why Gretchen?"

"It's Gretch-el. And why not?"

Diana was quiet, and Graham could tell she was considering the question. "I don't know. I just... She just... There's just something about her. About all these women," she said softly, reflectively. Then she abruptly shook out her bob. "Just tell me what you've learned." She was weary and frustrated.

She followed Graham toward the beige bedroom. Graham shivered at the doorway when he remembered Gretchel's telling of the rape. "I'm not sleeping in there."

"Why? All our stuff's in *there*."

"I'll move it out tomorrow. Next bedroom please."

Diana growled, and proceeded down the hall toward the guest bedroom. Graham peeked in, and figured that it had been Ame's room. He smiled, ran and dove onto the new bed. He flipped his naked body over, and rested on an elbow. Diana considered the pose. His hair was wild, and his beard was... Well she was ready to see that thing gone. He did resemble the Great God Pan. It was disconcerting. She felt a panicky tremor run through her, and then she carried on.

Graham smiled all the while.

"So spill it. Tell me about Gretchen?" Diana asked, as she refocused and methodically prepared for bed.

"It's Gretch-el. She's brilliant, but she's lost on a hero's journey, and I am incredibly blessed to be involved."

"A hero's journey?" Diana asked incredulously. "My mother is probably rolling over in her grave right now!"

"I've never seen you so jealous. My god, Miranda would have loved to have studied and helped Gretchel. It would have been a dream come true!"

"She was a transpersonal psychologist not a miracle worker. My father would have detested her."

Graham shook his head. "Charles Stewart would have felt the same as your mother. Your father was obsessed with uncovering the secrets of the psyche, but not for his own mind. He funded that research knowing it would help somebody in your care someday."

Diana knew that much was true. Her father had always spoken about how important their research was for Diana's future, and she never really understood why.

"I won't argue with that, and I'm sure a portion of their research will help me tremendously. But in case you missed the past forty years while flying about in Never Neverland, Peter Pan, that kind of research and testing is outlawed, so it's of no use to me now. Oh, that girl makes me feel like *I'm* going insane!"

"Just put your prejudices aside. If you truly want to unravel this mystery then you had better get off your pedestal and turn in the Queen Bee badge because there's a new girl in town, and she's the star of this show, not you."

"You're in love with her," she stated.

"Hopelessly," he answered with a dreamy smile.

"Don't attach yourself, Graham. It's dangerous. *She's* dangerous. I can step back for Eli's sake. I can do that to fulfill my end of the bargain, but I can't watch her toy with the men in my life. If she puts either one of you in danger, I may put her in six feet under."

Graham cackled. "Such big threats from such a tiny

sprite," he smiled. He pulled his wife down on the bed, and nibbled at her neck.

Diana pushed him away.

"So what did she tell you?" she grumpily persisted.

"Well for starters, she indeed has had four pregnancies."

"One of the two is still living or did live for a while, of that I can almost guarantee. It would make Ame the twenty-first descendent. Good work Graham, good work! Go on, go on."

He told her the story of Gretchel's marital rape. He could sense Diana taking on a whole new outlook, perhaps even sympathetic, and she planned to smudge and seal off the master bedroom first thing in the morning.

"The neighbor that helped her–Cody–do you think he still lives in this neighborhood?" Diana asked. Graham shrugged. "I saw dealer plates on a car across the street, that must be the blonde's house, the one she wanted you to give her lovely message to."

"Right. I just have a feeling the blonde may have a little inside information. Biased I'm sure, but information nonetheless. Oh! And Gretchel knows about the box, and has seen it in a vision."

"Oh good work Graham!" Diana celebrated.

"She doesn't know where it's at or what's in it, and wants nothing to do with it."

"Well it may be time to convince her otherwise. Opening that box–as dangerous as it may be–will set this family cycle straight. Why would she want to prohibit that?"

Graham shrugged. "Maybe the Woman in Wool

does."

"Most likely they both have a payoff by keeping it closed. I've got figure out the common bond."

"Let it go for now, Diana, and be kind tomorrow at the Beltane celebration. It's a big day for all of them. Gretchel absolutely needs to freely celebrate. She's come full circle."

She ignored him. "Did she reveal anything else? Did you notice anything odd, out of the ordinary?"

"Everything about that woman is out of the ordinary, but there was one thing you might find interesting if not disturbing."

Diana's eyes lit up. "What? What is it?"

Graham's heart sank. "Do you truly find joy in her adversities?"

"I have no reason not to."

"Compassion's never been your strength has it, love?"

"You care enough for both of us, now what in the hell can be more disturbing than being raped and beaten with a pitching wedge?" she asked.

"It's not *more* disturbing, just disturbing. Have you seen the horse, Epona?"

"Yes. I saw her briefly the first day I arrived."

"And what color is that horse?"

"White. White as snow."

"Not according to Gretchel," Graham said.

CHAPTER NINE
Irvine, 2010s

Gretchel woke early, though groggily the next morning. Gazing into the bathroom mirror, she felt the guilt monster trying to bubble up to the surface. With great effort, she pushed it back down. It quickly returned when she entered the kitchen and saw a mess of powered sugar and food coloring. The memory of the prior evening became clear in her mind.

She'd smoked weed. With her hero. She'd smoked weed with her hero.

As guilty as she felt, a grin slowly grew on her face. She quickly, if not clumsily, shuffled down to the basement, rummaged through some boxes and found an old journal. Inside was a 'to-do in my life' list that she'd made when she lived at the House on Pringle. She sifted through the pages, and scanned the list until she found *#48: Get high with G.O.D.* Check. If that was possible maybe *#1: Forgiving myself* would be too.

Never!

Gretchel slammed the journal shut. No need inviting

the Woman in Wool so early in the morning. She shuddered, and resolved right then and there to never touch marijuana again. It reminded her too much of booze, and that was a road she couldn't travel ever again. Her recovery would have to exclude pot. Period. The end. Silly as it seemed, it did make one thirsty, anyway.

She felt shame, but not nearly as much as she did when she thought of being caught flirting with Graham so openly. She cursed herself, thinking of all the times she drooled about Graham Duncan to Eli. She thought about the crush she still had on him, and how she must never exercise her desire, even if she had the freedom to do so.

She had been a sexual deviant in her past, and she knew it. "I may never be a normal person even if I am exorcised of this demon, and why would I want to be?"

Aye. The mad rocket's found one madder. Lad looks familiar? she heard a voice giggle in her head.

He's pure mental, and he be weasln ina nooks and crannies none get reach. Devil's bride 'll have her hide fer that to be sure.

Too much blether'n for mah taste. Ah'll wager the auld man has 'er moanin' by the next moon.

Ah'll take that wager.

Aye! Don't waste yer breath, this madbit's...

"Goddamn it, would you shut up?" Gretchel growled. She clenched her fists as hard as she could, and soon the voices died out.

Then it occurred to her that she didn't hear the voices even a little when she was with Graham. *Could he possess the same healing magic as Eli?* she wondered. She felt it plausible, and she suddenly wanted to know more about the Duncans. Maybe she wanted to be saved by Graham. He was her hero after all.

She walked into the backyard, and was greeted by an exuberant, but still noisy, Suzy-Q. The dog barked and whined running halfway back and forth from the Wicked Garden.

"No. Stop it girl. You're going to wake everyone, and there's no way in hell I'm going back toward that truck."

Suzy-Q reluctantly gave up the fight, and followed Gretchel further into the backyard. Following a Beltane ritual, Gretchel used dew from the freshly-cut grass to wipe upon her face. The short broken grass blades stuck, and she left them there as a tribute to the Green Man.

She looked out into the countryside, and thanked the green nature entity and the Goddess. She offered gratitude for her shelter, for the food she consumed, for the farm that had sustained her family for close to a century, for her children that continued to grow healthy and strong, for the rain that nourished the ground and for the earth that gave her everything. This portion of the earth was as sacred to her as it was to her Grand Mama. It was holy, and she treated it as such.

Onward to the lake she went. She sat on the edge of the island, one of her favorite spots in the world, and made an offering to Carlin: fresh strawberries, homemade bread, that Cindy had baked, and a handful of sage.

"Mo ghaol ort." Gretchel whispered the Scottish blessing to the water. *My love is with you.*

In a meditation trance, she observed the ripples. She was at peace.

The offerings that had been floating on top of the water disappeared piece by piece. Gretchel smiled. She moved closer in hopes of catching a glimpse of the fish that was nipping at the bread. She noticed movement, but there were no fish. She leaned in even closer.

"Oh gods!" she yelped.

A face–beautiful but scarred–floated to the surface. Gretchel jumped back and crouched defensively. In all her years at Snyder Farms she had never come face to face with the lady of the lake, and now she was looking her in the eye.

"Whit's fur ye'll no go by ye…"

The voice was ethereal. It echoed above and below. It enveloped the air all around Gretchel. She felt it in her soul. The visage remained a death mask, but comfort came from her voice.

Gretchel bowed before the ghostly figure. "Help me Carlin. Help me help you," she begged.

"Prepare for the Solstice," Carlin whispered, and then the image of Gretchel's great grand mama faded, and only a ripple remained.

Tears ran down Gretchel's face. She looked up to see the precious Goddess of Dawn making her grand arrival. Colors of pink, purple, yellow and orange dazzled in the May sky. Gretchel lay on the dock watching the natural air show. She wept. Through broken sobs, she asked the dawn for forgiveness, as was her routine nearly every morning.

The emotional pain was raw, unequalled and unbearable. A physical ache, hot and searing spread over her abdomen. Then she did what she always did when the pain got to be too much. She just ran away from it all. Suzy-Q, even more energetic than normal that morning, ran hard and pushed Gretchel to go further and deeper into the countryside, until she could run hard no more.

∞

Gretchel returned from her run, wonderfully exhausted and emotionally revivified. The image of her great grand mama was seared into the forefront of her mind. *And what in the hell is going to happen on the Solstice?* she wondered. The ancestors had spoke of the Solstice too. It was the one-day of the year she would gladly forget if she could.

She stepped into the barn, and noticed Eli lifting weights, as he often did.

"You've been crying. What's wrong?" he asked immediately. Gretchel touched at her puffy face. She was in no mood to revisit the wounds now.

"I'm fine. Sometimes I cry when I run. It's therapy. But thank you for asking and for taking such good care of me," she smiled appreciatively and quickly changed the subject to his bare-chested workout. "You look tasty this morning."

"Tastier than the green frosting you had last night?" he murmured.

"Much tastier," she replied.

She playfully slugged him in his rock hard gut. He feigned injury falling back on the bench. He instantly pulled himself back up, and tilted his head in confusion at Suzy-Q who ran into the barn and began barking fiercely. Eli did his best to ignore her.

"You know there's a reason I get up and work out just before you get back from running every morning," Eli said, still eyeballing the Saluki.

"Really?" Gretchel asked, and then turned to her dog. "Suzy-Q shut up or I'll drop you like a sack of taters!" she yelled. She turned back to Eli. "Continue."

Eli made a peculiar face, and then decided not to comment on her minor outburst. "It's so I can get a glimpse of you in those running pants. Turn around and let me get a closer look." She did, but stayed a good distance from him. "Yes, very nice. Very, very nice," he grinned mischievously.

She turned back around, and stared off toward Suzy-Q who was pacing the barn.

"What are you thinking about Gretchel? Another philosophical conundrum?"

"No. Just thinking how much needs to get done today."

He reached out and pulled her down onto his lap. "Tomorrow you and I are going to take a long ride on the Harley and get away from all of this madness."

"Can't wait. Will you hook me up with some assless chaps?" she teased.

"Boy will I," he smiled in delight. "Don't forget we're going to St. Louis Wednesday for at least a few days. It's part of the gift I promised."

"Oh gods! I did forget! I forgot all about it. I need to pack! What are we doing there? What do I need to take?"

Eli closed his eyes as Gretchel's obsessive panic ensued. "Forget it for now, Gretchel. You have enough to deal with today. Now what do you want me to do? I'm your obedient slave."

"I like the sound of that," she laughed, running the hands through his hair just enough to tease him before she moved into command mode. "Set up the tables, the chairs and the Maypole. Finish hanging the twinkly lights and the garland, and then get the hell out of here. I don't want to see you or your trouble-making parents until later for prom pictures."

"Well I thought maybe I'd take my dad fishing this afterno..."

"No! He's too much of a distraction. I can't work while he's around, I can barely talk when he's around."

"Not much talking get done last night then?"

She smacked his shoulder. "Of course we talked, we talked a lot, but that's beside the point, I'm not stoned or hypnotized today. I have to focus!"

"Will you be okay by yourself?"

She glared at him. "I am intrigued by your healing energy and presence Eli, but we cannot coexist if you are up my ass all the time. I am willing to take the chance that the Woman in…"

"Don't say it!" he warned.

"My mama and grand mama will be around all day, and I am willing to take the chance that the evil voice in my head may show up. They will know how to handle her. And something tells me she won't show herself to Miss Poni anyway." *I dare her.*

CHAPTER TEN
Irvine, 2010s

Gretchel wanted so desperately to tell Teddy and Miss Poni about Carlin's appearance, and she also wanted to know if the crone would share any psychic insights about what was going to occur on the Solstice. But the time wasn't quite right to delve into that madness. There was work to be done, and Gretchel was a worker. She always worked hard. And at one time she played hard too, but that was ancient history. Gretchel was not alone in her labors. All the Witches of Snyder Farms cooked, cleaned, decorated and laughed until early afternoon.

Marcus, nursing a hangover, prepared a wooden teepee-like structure in the center of the backyard. To everyone's delight, Gretchel had approved the burning of a bon fire.

Marcus's son Blake, who was a master's student at SIU-C had sent her a text saying he and his girlfriend Hannah were on their way. She sent Brody a text, and he replied saying his girlfriend, Chloe, had a car at U of I where and they would be there soon.

All was going according to Gretchel's master plan, all except for Suzy-Q who barked incessantly. She would jump on Gretchel, then run to the Wicked Garden, and then run back. Gretchel was on the verge of a whole new level of insanity by the time Ame and Holly left with Cindy to be made over for prom.

Gretchel finally gave herself over to self-care, with a long relaxing shower. She savored the feeling of the water as it washed the stress off her body. It was sensual. It had been two days since she'd had sexual intercourse, which was abnormal since Eli had arrived, and she felt the longing grow inside of her. She realized it was probably her new cycle driving the need.

She slipped on a pair of teal printed hot pants, and a white top that clung to her chest. She looked in the mirror, and for the first time in a long time she liked what she saw. She felt sexy, powerful and much like the Aphrodite she knew she was or, at least, had been. She waited for a voice of some sort to make an off-color comment, but she heard nothing. She smiled at herself, and touched the new mirror lovingly.

Everyone had left the cottage to prepare themselves for the evening, but Gretchel, not surprisingly, refused to go to the salon or anywhere near Irvine. So as unheard of as it was and especially on prom day, Eli paid Stephen, Teddy's partner, double to make a house call.

"Teddy's worried about you Gretchel. He's worried sick," Stephen said.

"Why is he worried? Eli's here, everything's fine now."

"Maybe that's why he's worried. When you say things are fine, that's usually code for: *I'm just barely hanging on*."

Stephen tied the long, red hair into a ponytail at the nape of her neck, then braided it loosely, and brought sporadic strands out. He fixed fresh white daisies down the braid, then worked in the delicate wreath she had made, at the crown of her head.

"Are you feeling okay?" he asked.

"I'm fine. I feel fine. Oh! You're trying to trick me! Look, I'll be honest with you Stephen, I've had a weird vibe ever since I woke up this morning."

"Is it a bad weird?"

"It's a mixed weird," she said, and wasn't about to confide in anyone, but Teddy or Miss Poni that she'd seen Carlin's ghost.

He finished the wreath and looked back at his creation. "You're a work of art once again, Gretchel. Now please be good to yourself. If you start feeling worse than weird, please tell someone. All you have to do is call or text if there's an emergency. Teddy and I will be back for the party later."

Stephen left her in peace, and just when she decided she might sit on the patio for a moment and enjoy the solitude, Peyton pulled into the drive.

"Ah shit," she said aloud.

Who knew how long she would be alone with the wretched little horn dog until someone returned. She greeted him awkwardly, and then showed him into the house, where he hung his tux in the bathroom.

They returned to the patio, and he stared at her, not talking, just staring. Her long legs were stretched out, and her bare feet crossed. Peyton gazed from the painted toes, all the way up to her tight shorts. He lingered on her chest, and then met her eyes. Gretchel stared back at him in utter amazement, as he ignored her irritation to begin the visual journey in reverse.

"How's school going?" she asked tapping her fingers on the table.

"Good."

She nodded, and twisted her lips with her fingers.

"I guess Ame told you all the big news around here, about Eli being her father and all."

"Yeah. I'm happy for her. Eli's a great guy."

"Yes, yes he is. Have big plans for the summer, Peyton?"

"Not really."

He continued the creepy assessment of her body. Gretchel sighed. *This is ridiculous!*

"Peyton follow me," she ordered aggressively. His eyes lit up, and she had to wonder what was going on in his head.

She led him to the cottage living room, and arrived at the place where the shotgun once sat. "I own a shotgun, Peyton, and I know how to use it. That's not a threat in any way, shape or form. It is a promise."

Peyton was rendered speechless with embarrassment.

"Respect me and respect yourself!" she screeched. "Stop gawking at me for crying out loud. Don't you like my daughter?"

"Yes. I love her," he said hoarsely.

"Well how do you think she would feel if she saw you right now goggling over me? Do you think you'd have a snowball's chance in hell of ever talking to her again?"

He shook his head no.

"I am not attracted to young men, especially when they date my daughter. Now go get your fucking tux on, and don't look at me again today unless I speak to you!" she shouted and pointed to the bathroom.

He rushed away, and shut the door behind him without looking back.

The things Aphrodite must do, Gretchel thought. She opened the kitchen door just as the girls pulled up. Eli followed in the Mercedes, then Graham and Diana in another car. *And my timing is getting better with age.*

Gretchel greeted Eli with a long kiss. "I missed you today," she smiled. "Did you stay busy?"

"Yeah," he chuckled. "Dad and I joined the country club."

"You're kidding me?"

"Nope. Picture this if you will, Gretchel: Graham Duncan went into the Irvine Country Club clubhouse wearing a bright orange sweatband around his curly mop, beard braided, wearing a thin nearly worn out white tank top, allowing his pornographic tattoos of Pan to be displayed. He had on cut off jean shorts and Birkenstocks. A pair of thirty-year-old Converse All Stars were slung over his shoulder and $1000 tennis racket in hand. He looked like a day-tripping John McEnroe. He slapped a credit card down and said he wanted a year membership and a six-pack of ice cold Budweiser. The clerk hesitated, obviously dumbstruck, and he repeated: *Ice. Cold.* Once that was squared away, we walked through the clubhouse that was shocked into a silence like you've never heard before. He spotted a blonde that was just a little too unnaturally perfect. He confidently walked up to her, and whispered the little *fuck-off-and-die* message you wanted him to share if he ever saw her. Well, Graham Duncan is a man of his word. The look on that woman's face was priceless. It was quite possibly the funniest thing I've ever seen. She was speechless. Then we went out to the courts and he kicked my ass in tennis while a group of about thirty people watched. Humility is my middle name."

Gretchel laughed madly, stomping her foot and slapping her leg. "Michelle Brown probably didn't know what hit her. He's brilliant."

"Brilliant or mentally ill... Shit. That came out wrong."

Gretchel rolled her eyes and pulled herself together. Still chuckling, she admired the newly arrived teenager's physical transformations. She glanced at Graham who was dressed in a dark brown pin striped suit with a purple and green paisley button-down shirt. A hunter green scarf was tied loosely around his neck and those damn worn out Birkenstocks were on his feet. His hair, the same sandy brown as Eli's, bore its many gray fragments gracefully and was disheveled in a way that made the butterflies in Gretchel's belly frolic in the most peculiar fashion. The most detailed accessory of all was the mischievous grin. Gretchel thought she might melt into the driveway.

The pendulum swung as she looked at Diana who was the complete opposite, put together to a tee in a classy tweed pastel Chanel suit and heels. What *did* these two have in common? She admired Diana's style, but she much preferred Graham's avant-garde get-up. It was playful and fun and humorous and jolly.

She greeted Ella and Miss Poni as they pulled in to the driveway next. They all walked around the cottage to see the completed masterpiece that was the Beltane backyard. There were accolades aplenty as Gretchel plugged in all the twinkly lights, just as Peyton walked onto the patio in his tux, and eyed the group like a deer caught in the headlights.

Gretchel made eye contact with him for a split second, and then quickly walked toward the Maypole. She noticed Graham fall into pace with her. "You've been naughty this afternoon," he whispered.

She didn't break her gate, but drew in a deep breath. "No. Peyton was naughty. I put him in his place. You were naughty too I hear."

"My naughtiness didn't involve my daughter's boyfriend."

"I did nothing wrong. I asserted my position, and how do you know anyway?" she whispered back.

"I can read you like a nudey mag, Kittycat, and it's turning me on something fierce," he responded

"Are you a dirty old man, Mr. Duncan? Because I'm beginning to get that vibe, and it's slightly unsettling," she replied just as Suzy-Q went crazy at the sight of Graham, and began barking and pacing sporadically again. Gretchel's hands began to shake, and she could feel the demon trying to fight her way into consciousness. Everything was happening too quickly, and she couldn't keep a grip on the moment, especially with the dog's obnoxious barking.

Meanwhile Peyton walked toward Amc, and she

smiled coyly. "Hey," she said.

"Hey," he responded. "I've missed you. A lot."

She kicked at the ground, and then threw her arms around him. "I've missed you too," she said, burying her face in his neck.

"I think you made a believer out of him," Graham whispered to Gretchel.

"Yes, my work here is done, but if this day gets any more stressful I may have to voluntarily check myself into Choate." She stopped suddenly, and screamed as loud as she could at the dog. "Shut the fuck up dog or I'll shoot you in the damn head!"

Everyone snapped their heads to Gretchel and became very, very quiet.

"Choate?" Graham asked carefully. "Isn't that the state mental home near Carbondale?"

"Yes sir," she replied, lowering her head and swinging her hair around to hide from all the faces that stared her way.

"Uh huh... And is the shot gun locked up, Honeylove?"

"Tighter than me as a preteen."

Blessed be, Graham thought, and walked her back to the group that had resumed its chattering.

Ame held Peyton's hand, and looked over the backyard that had been transformed into a fairy playground. She had her family, her boyfriend and now this glorious sight. She was beside herself with ambivalence. She finally stomped her flip-flopped foot and proclaimed: "I don't want to go to the prom!"

Eli looked at Gretchel with wide eyes. All the work

they'd done on the dress, and now this. *Oh Ame, don't push her today.*

Gretchel looked like she might blow a gasket. "Get your ass in that house, and get dressed before I lose it!" she screamed. She marched Ame toward the cottage. Cindy and Holly followed.

"I've never seen anyone so bossy and temperamental," Diana mumbled.

Eli shook his head, exhausted by hypocrisy.

CHAPTER ELEVEN
Irvine, 2010s

Eli followed Gretchel into the their bedroom. She frantically searched the room.

"Where's my clipboard?" she growled.

"I saw it outside. Please stop rushing yourself. Why don't you rest before you get dressed for the party."

She ignored him. Eli playfully picked her up, and dumped her on the bed. He beamed as he stared down at her, trying to pretend all was well and that he wasn't on edge, though he'd been told about the rape that day.

"Rest!" he commanded.

"Is that an order, Mr. Stewart? Uh, wait you're not a Green or a Stewart. You're a Duncan," she said.

"Yes. I am a Duncan. I'm a Stewart to be sure, but in my heart I am and always will be a Duncan. Now that you know, make sure you never forget it, Gretchel. Now rest."

For some reason Gretchel knew it *was* very important that she not forget. He was a mixture of both his mother and father, though much more like his father, and she thanked the Goddess for that. He was a younger version of Graham physically, and he was light, gentle and playful like Graham just not to the masculine extreme. But he had a reserved side of him like Diana, a darker side that showed in his eyes when he was thinking too hard or worried. It was the side she'd seen in him when he was ready to tear Troy apart in Carbondale, but didn't.

He released her, turned himself around, and she snuck off the bed.

"You're not fooling me, Gretchel. Just please rest."

"I have too much on my mind," she whined, and rubbed her temples.

"Well let it go," he said, stripping off his jeans in exchange for a pair of pressed dark gray chinos. "Tonight is about fun. *'And the night shall be filled with music, And the cares that infest the day, Shall fold their tents, like the Arabs, and silently steal away.'*"

"Eli, that was beautiful. Did you just think of it?" she asked.

He laughed. "If only. It's Longfellow."

"I like it," she said appreciatively. "But I can't rest; I'll mess up the wreath and my hair."

Eli looked over Stephen's beautiful creation. Gretchel looked like an original flower child. He wanted to take her into the woods and... and... He shook the libidinous thoughts from his head.

"We wouldn't want to mess up the hair," he said softly. "It's beautiful. I can't wait to see what you're going to wear." He tried to kiss her, but she pushed him away.

"I'm getting ready," she smiled. "Close your eyes."

Gretchel went to her closet, while Eli blindly buttoned a white shirt, and slipped on a charcoal sweater and a blazer.

"Okay. You can look."

Eli gasped, and fell back on the bed.

"What?"

"You're trying to bewitch me again, Gretchel Bloome." She gave him an all too familiar eye roll.

"Where did you get that dress?" he asked.

It was a beautiful sage green. The neckline plunged in an accentuated V past her breasts where beige lacing held them in place. Beige trim and intricate swirly stitching bordered the V and the edge of the flowing sleeves. Her breasts sat perfectly behind the fitted bodice, and her cleavage made an appearance behind beige ties. It flowed down her curvy frame, and ended at her ankles where more intricate detail surrounded the angled cut of the bottom.

"I made it. I made this and another dress for the Summer Solstice party before you even came back to Illinois. I had a lot of time to fill, and I can't waste time."

"I sleep with a goddess."

"Well that would mean I sleep with a god, and that makes sense, because I've raised my standards and I simply refuse to sleep with mortal men any more," she said, and smiled coyly. She let him hold her, and she lovingly massaged his neck with her long fingers.

Eli's throat felt curiously dry.

"So now I'm a god?" he said hoarsely. He nuzzled her ear, and breathed in the delectable strawberry scent of her skin that never failed to leave him woozy, and it somewhat soothed the scratchiness in his throat.

"Of course. You always were, but not a Celtic god, you'll always be Hermes to me."

"Always the messenger. You know Hermes had other duties, he was Aphrodite's lover for one," he said and kissed her forehead. "He was a psychopomp too."

Gretchel's thumbs pressed in on his voice box, and her fingers squeezed his neck tight. She was strangling him.

"Gretchel... Stop it! You're... Hurting me!" He pried her hands off, and then noticed the glazed look in her eyes. "Gretchel!"

He shook her hard, until she came back from wherever she had been.

It took her a few moments to come to, and then she whispered an apology. A horrible feeling thundered in the pit of Eli's stomach. "Show me your other creation," he said trying to avert her attention and deny her murderous actions.

She went to her closet, and pulled out the other dress. Eli thought he might pass out. His heartbeat quickened, his stomach rolled and sweat beaded on his forehead. "You made it for your birthday?" he asked.

"No. I made it for the Summer Solstice party, which happens to land on my birthday, which I *do not* want to celebrate this year, by the way. I saw the dress in a dream or a nightmare. I'm not sure which. I just knew I had to create it." It was a beautiful flowing ivory gown with gold detail.

Eli couldn't speak; he only nodded, and swallowed the bile that was trying to force its way up. He had seen the dress before too, but it had been in a vision on the cottage lake over seventeen years prior.

∞

Eli sat on the deck fiddling with his camera equipment. He occasionally glanced at Gretchel meandering around the yard. She was stunning. He wanted to take picture after picture of his love in the beautiful sage dress, but the terror of her trying to choke him was looping like a loose film in his head. She hadn't been teasing. He knew she was under the influence of a force beyond her control. As physically strong a man as he was, he had no idea how to fight ghosts. He had no idea how to protect Gretchel... or himself for that matter. Protection was out of his hands at this point.

Lenses changed, Eli glanced down and saw Holly below the deck looking right back up at him. She had been smudging the perimeter of the cottage. When her eyes met Eli's she dropped her smudge wand and bundle of white sage. She was frozen, and looked to not be present in her body, just as Gretchel had behaved.

Eli jutted down the steps, and put his hand on her back. "Holly, are you okay?" he asked.

She looked him in the eye, but it wasn't Holly, someone else was speaking through the young medium. "You're the one I saw in my vision. You look just like I imagined. She should have stayed home like I told her." The voice didn't even sound like Holly, but it clearly came from her mouth.

Eli thought his heart might stop beating. He felt a hand on his shoulder, and jumped. It was Miss Poni. "If you could retrieve Holly's tools from the ground, she can finish her duties. This property could use some extra protection tonight, don't you think?"

Holly quickly finished her work, and met up with her boyfriend, Dylan, to prepare for pictures. Eli hadn't even noticed she was already dressed for the prom. She was beautiful. The robin egg blue contrasted beautifully with her long red hair. She was a demure creature, timid and talented. He'd heard her play piano and knew she was quite studious. From what he'd heard, her clairvoyant skills were very strong, and he was starting to wonder if she had even more talents in that area that no one was aware of, or at least was not sharing.

The poor girl was terribly shy, and not comfortable being fussed over by her brothers, parents and grand mamas. She wasn't used to receiving so much attention. The attention always belonged to Ame. Eli made a note to get to know the girl better. She seemed to be a harbinger of warnings, and Eli needed to be able to decipher her codes. Maybe Ame could help. He searched the yard for his newly discovered offspring.

"Seen Ame?" he asked Gretchel.

"She's bringing Epona around. She wants to be photographed with that ridiculous black night mare," Gretchel scowled.

Eli looked at his mother who stood behind Gretchel. Diana was making a swirly crazy motion with her finger to her temple, and Graham quickly slapped her hand down.

What the hell? Eli wondered. *That horse is white.*

"Holly let me see you," Gretchel chirped. "Oh my goodness, you are stunning!"

Holly stood in front of everyone, and the crowd

clapped, but as routine, her moment in the sun didn't last long. Suddenly the sun found its true object of affection and proceeded to reflect light off shiny red flowing strands of hair that was atop the natural center of attention. She came walking slowly out of the barn, barefoot, in her prom dress. The six foot three, seventeen-year-old bombshell rendered the entire group speechless.

Ame's dress was a traffic stopper, and fit her perfectly. It was ivory and strapless, with a tight bodice that held up her full chest, and bared just enough cleavage to be daring yet stylish. The bodice was tight all the way down to hug her curves, and a chiffon skirt flowed behind her as she walked. A slit went up her right thigh, revealing a long, athletic leg that just could not possibly be real. The intricate beadwork, that took so many hours to complete, covered the bodice, and trimmed the entire skirt. It shone like the sun like diamonds.

Ame guided Epona gracefully across the yard, and smiled at the group. Diana actually sprouted tears, and she hugged Eli around his waist. "This is one of the happiest and most unexpected moments of my life," she cried.

"Now that's saying something," Graham smirked. Eli shook his head at his father in agreement.

"What's wrong with you people?" Ame asked, in typical Ame fashion.

"We're stunned by your magnificence pumpkin-puss. You are truly a goddess manifested, and I bow down to your divinity," Graham said, and kneeled before her.

"You have got to be kidding me," she laughed, and with her left arm pulled him back up. Their eyes met, and something odd ran through the pair as Ame held tight to Epona's reign. It was a gut feeling, a feeling that they should both know by now what their roles were.

Peyton stepped in, and lightly stroked Ame's arm. "You're smokin'," was all the boy could say.

Suddenly Epona was tugging and pulling Ame away from the group.

"What's that crazy beast doing?" Gretchel asked in obvious irritation, just as Suzy-Q revived her conniption fit, barking like mad.

Something eerie was transpiring in Graham's head, like his pituitary gland was being clouted with a jester's scepter insisting that he listen. It was the psychic clown again. "Follow Epona's lead. Let her guide you."

"No!" Gretchel shouted. "We have to get pictures. We're running out of time. Suzy-Q shut the fuck up!"

"Baby Girl, watch your language or I'm gonna smack you silly," Ella growled.

Gretchel grabbed at her head. *Kill the psychopomps. Kill the psychopomps.*

Eli whispered to her. "Sweetheart, put your mental clipboard away for a minute and try to go with the flow like you talked about." She shot him a dirty look.

Ame looked at Graham for permission to follow Epona. He winked and egged her on, and so she allowed herself to be lead by the horse. They all watched as Epona walked back toward the barn, and into the Wicked Garden with Suzy-Q going absolutely berserk by their side.

"I don't like this Eli, it's making me feel sick. We

have to start pictures. Holly's date is going to be here soon," Gretchel complained. Eli tried to calm her with a finger on her lips. She swatted it down.

Diana quickly pulled a small video camera from her purse, and hit record.

Gretchel grabbed at her head again. *Kill the psychopomps. Kill the psychopomps,* was the mantra.

She was doing everything she could to keep herself in control. Graham saw her discomfort, took her hand away from Eli, and they slowly followed Ame, the horse and the dog, while the others stayed several steps behind.

The horse led Ame to the front of the truck, and she gasped.

"What is it?" Gretchel cried.

The voice screamed in her head: *Kill the psychopomps! Kill the psychopomps!* Gretchel was unaware that she had stepped into the perimeter of the Wicked Garden. The moment she did, the voice was silenced.

"Oh my god!" Ame yelled, waving the crowd forward.

The group rushed to the front of the truck.

There, in the middle of a chaotic mix of weeds was a single, bright, orange-red poppy. Blooming.

Gretchel instantly grew soft, serene, and her smile was undeniable. Eli pushed his father out of the way, and very delicately touched Gretchel's back. She jerked. "Are you in shock or awe?"

"I'm fine."

What kind of answer is that? Eli wondered.

Miss Poni, with Cindy's assistance, finally reached the scene. Tears began flowing down the crone's face as soon as she caught sight of the flower.

"It's been over eighty years since a poppy has bloomed in this garden," she said, wiping tears away. "It's a sign. It's a sign from my mama."

Ella and Cindy both wrapped their arms around Miss Poni. Cindy looked around the garden. "Did you feel that?" she asked.

Ella and Miss Poni nodded. They felt it all right. Everyone in the group felt a wave of tingles wash over them, and quickly disappear as a light spring breeze lifted their hair, as if a door was swinging open.

"The veil's been lifted," Miss Poni said.

Gretchel walked to the passenger side of the truck, where normally the energy was tragic and heavy. But today is was peaceful. "I can feel her, Mama," Gretchel said. She touched the truck door and smiled. "She's here."

"Who? Who is here? Who do you mean?" Eli implored.

Her other child would be my guess, son, Diana thought. Her eyes were wide as she focused on Gretchel and the truck.

Graham, however, had his eyes on Holly. The timid girl peered at nothing, as if she were in a trance. Graham tapped Diana's elbow.

"Holly what's wrong?" Ame whispered. "Do you see something?"

"We're all here now," Holly replied blankly.

"Who?" Ame asked. Diana zoomed in her video camera, but couldn't quite make out what the girls were saying

"The psychopomps," Holly whispered to her cousin.

"What the hell are you talking about?" Ame pleaded. Then a memory came barreling into Ame's consciousness. It was of the talk she'd had with Eli in the barn earlier that spring. *Psychopomps can travel to the underworld in safety.* After a little online research, she learned that psychopomps were soul guides. The goddess Epona was a psychopomp. Ame suddenly held tighter to Epona's reign.

"Holly, are you one of the psychopomps?" Ame begged quietly.

"Yes, and we're all in grave danger."

Whit's fur ye'll no go by ye.

Part Two

Atlantic Ocean, 1600s

Curstaidh had just turned fourteen when she traveled with her mother to Eire. Tragedy had befallen her little family, and her mother was anxious to get away. Young Curstaidh welcomed the change and was curious about the new land.

Her father had suddenly fallen ill, and passed away soon after. He was a beast of a man, whom Curstaidh had despised. He had not been good to her or her mother, Myrna. Curstaidh was not sorry her father was gone, nor for how he passed. She was sure her mother had welcomed in the sickness with her magic. Her mother was no stranger to guilt, but now it took on an even grander tone, almost as if she'd been cursed as a result.

Curstaidh watched her mother fret day and night. Myrna had nightmares, making it intolerable for Curstaidh to sleep on most occasions. It was an evening such as this, as they sailed to the new land, that she met an old man with aquamarine eyes.

She stood at the edge of the ship and gazed across a vast ocean. It was just too large for her to comprehend.

The full moon was a massive gold coin in the rare, clear sky, and the reflection of light on the water was the only thing separating the elements, her and Eire.

Curstaidh sensed company. She turned to see the man sitting to her right. He had been scratching words into a leather book, when he looked up and smiled. Her mama had instructed her many times not to speak to strange men, especially since she'd been caught doing so (and often more than talking) time after time with boys from their village. Myrna feared that it would be her daughter's downfall if she did not take heed of the warnings and tame herself. Curstaidh understood her mother's fear, but she presently sensed that this old man meant her no harm.

"Guid eenin! Have ye ever felt tiny and enormous all at once?" she asked the man. He was a peculiar looking fellow. She guessed him to be nearing the end of his days, as his hair was white and wild and his face was wrinkled by sun and time. He looked weary, as if he had been traveling for a very long time. Curstaidh thought she could see huge sorrow in his eyes, though he smiled as if he had much grace in his heart.

"Aye. Quite often, lass. Those moments I can feel the gods within me. I find those moments to be quite joyous."

Curstaidh grinned broadly. She had found a kindred spirit. "Then why do ye look so sad?" She pointed to the moon. "The Goddess lights yer pages, the water and air move ye to yer next destination. Ye've much to be thankin' the lady fer."

The man chuckled. "Aye. So I do. What brings ye out into the cold night, young one? Was the Goddess keeping ye awake with her soulshine?"

Curstaidh laughed. She found his voice and his way with words delightful. "Nah, it was mah mama. She's restless and dreams of a night mare. And she dreams of *her* mama drowning before her very eyes and of heartache and fire. It keeps mah eyes from closing fer slumber. We've seen hard times, we have. I keep mah smile fer her, and fer this hope in mah heart of a better way."

"Yer mama is fortunate to have ye fer her child."

"Aye, but she cannae see past her misery," the girl said quietly, and kicked at the side of the boat. "Mama worships a box that burns us to the touch. She willnae let it go. Says mah grand mama willnae let her."

"But yer grand mama's passed?" the man asked.

"Aye! Mama's head's turn'n to mince. We keep the box in a sack to keep from touching it. The box is pretty to see, but has a droch feeling we cannae be near for long. A'm ready to be free of it. Mama says keeping it will free me some day. She says it will free her and my grand mama too. Sometimes I wonder if she's gone mad, like the grand mama I never knew."

The man was thoughtful as he watched the young girl. Her hair was long, and the light wind made it dance on her back. He could see the red strands sparkle in the moonlight. It reminded him of days gone by. They were the days he wrote about, and couldn't seem to let be.

"Are ye a bard?" Curstaigh asked loudly to change the subject. "I like to scratch the quill myself. Mama says it's mah gift. I had to hide it from mah pa, but no more. He's gone now, and A'm better fer it. What do ye write about? Ye look like ye've seen hard times yerself.

Is that what ye scratch about? What have ye seen with those magical blue eyes a yers?" Curstaigh asked the haggard soul.

The man guffawed. The girl was tickling him, and for the first time in ages he found true joy in the company of a woman, though she was young enough to be his granddaughter.

"I write of love and loss. I write of heroes and villains. Of kings and castles. Of the green valleys of the homeland and the taste of my one and only true love's sweet lips. I also write of another woman who was not mah love, but was a good wife who lost her life in childbirth, and of mah brave son I raised alone. I write of a mother I miss and a father I honor. I write of the sea and the clan of mah ancestors. I write of the old ways. I write of the new ways. And I write of *mah* ways. I write about redheaded beauties being saved. I write of death and of life and of salvation. I write of joy and sadness. I write of witches and curses and the men I would gladly kill was I blessed to see them again. I write of a torturous melancholy and regret that seizes me up in the middle 'o the night, sending me to the side of a boat to chat with curious young lassies. I write of truth and I write of lies. I make up what I want to read and I lose mahself in these words. I write happy endings always, because I believe in the circle. That is what I scratch about, young one. I write what is in mah head. I write to get it out so that I willnae toss myself o're the boat to become dinner for the sea. There is no honor in that sort 'o death. Remember that child. Donnae let yer grandmother's end become yer legacy."

Curstaigh was entranced, completely captivated.

She'd never met a man with this kind of charisma. "Mama says she still hears mah grand mama. It scares mah some days. How can the story of someone ye never knew scare ye?"

"Aye. Well don't let a ghost scare ye 'til ye've seen one yerself. Courage young one. Ye've got courage. I can see it in ye."

Curstaigh smiled humbly. The man went back to his writing spot, and picked up his brown, leather satchel. He opened it, and Curstaigh took a quick glance inside to see a collection books. "Did ye fill all those with yer own words?"

"I did." He reached inside the bag and pulled out a clean specimen. "Mah gift to ye young one. May ye fill it with all the pleasantries of yer life, well-lived."

Curstaigh gave him with a hearty embrace. "Thenk ye…Whit's yer name…"

"They call me the messenger."

CHAPTER TWELVE
Irvine, 2010s

The enthusiastic discovery of the mystical poppy was halted by the arrival of Beltane guests. Eli rushed through a less than organized prom photo shoot, while Gretchel nipped at his ankles to hurry. Eli was *trying* to hurry, but was continually distracted by the concerned look on Ame's face. It was deeming her less than photogenic.

"Eli, I need to talk to you," she tried when he finished the shoot, but she was interrupted by a synchronized tug from Peyton and Gretchel.

"Ame, you have reservations. You have to go!" Gretchel snapped.

Eli wrapped her in a quick embrace. "Wake me up when you get home, Ame-with-an-E. Stop worrying and have fun," he whispered.

After greeting the many guests of farmhands, family friends and commercial farm acquaintances, Eli and Gretchel joined Diana and Graham at the head table. The Stewart-Duncans were honored guests. Miss Poni, Ella and her friend, Thomas, were also among those at the head table.

It was a lively group, and the entire crowd seemed to be sharing the joyous vibe that had not been prevalent at the farm for many years. Diana would have shared the joy if she weren't so busy watching Gretchel with a hard analytical eye. *She's just too aesthetically perfect. That's the problem. She's just too perfect, and too damn ungrateful for her perfection.* She felt little but contempt for the mother of her only grandchild.

Diana looked around the table and wondered who in their right mind decided it would be a good idea to sit Graham next to Miss Poni. *They'll be carrying on like the Mad Hatter and the March Hare before the end of dinner,* she thought.

She considered the information Graham had retrieved from Gretchel the night before. He'd gotten information out of her fairly easily, but Diana had to wonder what Gretchel could still be hiding that was worse than what she'd already shared. It had to be about the two other children she'd conceived. She saw no other possibility.

Diana's eyes darted to Eli. *Good grief!* The boy looked pale, sick as a dog. *What the hell is wrong with him?* Her thoughts were interrupted as Graham filled her wine glass. He'd had a case shipped up from Alto-Pass, a region near Carbondale, rich with wineries.

"Merry be, my love," Graham whispered in her ear. He poked at her ribs. "Start drinking or I will tickle you mercilessly."

She gave him a sneer. Then she sipped at the wine. She nodded with surprised approval. "It's good," she said. "It's very, very good."

That settles that, Graham thought, as he sat the bottle of wine in front of his wife. *The little troublemaker can be drunk and merry today.* He glanced across the table at Gretchel and winked. She pursed her pouty lips, and the freckles on her cheeks instantly flooded with a chagrinned blush.

Graham sighed. *Oh my, my, my. This woman just has no idea what she's capable of. No idea.* He glimpsed the soft white skin of her cleavage as she reached out for her glass of sweet iced tea. Graham shuddered as a cold chill ran through him. Gretchel was flipping his world upside down and inside out, and there was nothing he enjoyed more.

He finished his salad, and then took notice of Eli. *Jiminy Cricket! He looks like the Grim Reaper with a saki hangover.*

"Aye. He doesn't look so good," Miss Poni remarked quietly.

Graham eyeballed the relic beside him. "Young lady, can you read my thoughts?"

Miss Poni smiled devilishly. "Just a few. The boy looks troubled."

"Indeed. He looks like he just walked out of a big budget horror movie."

"Chances are pretty good he's living one."

Graham chuckled. He found Miss Poni to be an unexpected treat. If he had to guess, he would say she had been a handful in her day too.

She slowly turned to look him in the eye, and

Graham felt a peculiar feeling wash through him.

"Miss Poni, you blazing ball of verve, do you know things about me that I don't know?"

"I know lots of things, child," she said. It had been a while since someone had called Graham a child without the use of unadulterated sarcasm.

"And are you at liberty to discuss any of the things you know?" he asked.

She smiled graciously, and lured him in with an old finger that vaguely resembled a fried chicken strip. He bent to listen. "Your father was pure of heart too."

Graham was speechless. The hair raised on his arms. Tears instantly glassed over his remarkable aqua eyes. His mother, Penelope, was the only one who had ever described the man that was his father. He had never come across anyone who knew the mysterious man called Dominic Duncan. Graham was beside himself with curiosity, but he held back out of respect. The crone would share more when she was ready. He took Miss Poni's hand and put it to his lips.

"Thank you," he whispered. "Your secret's safe with me."

"Your wife seems quite intent on digging up secrets. Why are you so trustworthy and composed, Mr. Duncan?"

"Because I have infinite patience, and what you've said is enough for now. It's enough to last me the rest of my life if necessary."

"It won't be. I will share much more with you. But your patience is honorable."

"Thank you," he humbly replied.

"Hmph..." The old woman crossed her arms, and

stared at the barn.

"What are you thinking about now, Miss Poni?" Graham grinned suspiciously, and then took a sip of wine.

"I was just wishing I were thirty years younger, so I could take you to the barn and give you a righteous, rowdy shagging."

A shower of wine blew out Graham's semi-closed lips. "Oh Miss Poni, let's get to work on that time machine ASAP."

∞

When she wasn't stealing glimpses at her hero, Graham Duncan, or rubbing Eli's leg under the table, Gretchel was looking around the yard at the magical scene that had been created. The lights, the flora and the soft Scottish music that played in the background were spellbinding. The sights, the smells, and the audio were all overwhelmingly soothing. She'd never felt so comfortable and at ease. Eli had been right; it was time to enjoy the fruits of her labor. Of course Suzy-Q's barking had come to a halt after she'd pointed out the blooming poppy, and that had helped considerably.

She gazed over the many people that had gathered for Beltane: Marcus and Cindy with Brody, Blake and their girlfriends. It was so good to have the boys back at Snyder Farms. She hadn't seen either of them since Troy's funeral in January, and that made her think of Zach. She missed him desperately, but couldn't allow herself to sink into dismay. She decided to focus on who was present.

She gazed at Teddy and Stephen's table full of laughter and charm. They sat with a few friends from the salon that Gretchel had grown to love, as well as Teddy's mother and stepfather.

Then there were the other tables full of Marcus's trusted friends, neighbors and farm employees. Gretchel could have invited so many more of her own friends. No. They weren't her friends. She had to keep reminding herself that they had all turned their back on her when Troy died. They were forced to pick sides between her and Michelle. *Was just as well,* she thought. She enjoyed her solitude at the cottage, and she didn't enjoy pretenses anyway. The only people she thought she needed were the ones that were celebrating Beltane. The ones that loved her even when she was a crazy fool.

∞

Eli barely touched his food, and it was a damn crying shame. The fresh spring salad, new potatoes, roasted asparagus, venison back strap, chocolate tart with fresh strawberries and Scottish oatcakes all looked so good earlier, but now the sight of food made his stomach ache worse. Gretchel looked hurt when his salad went untouched, but when he pushed around his main course, he could tell she was almost in tears. He finally began eating, though it was definitely forced.

He was worried about Gretchel's sanity again. He knew to listen to his body, he knew to trust his intuition, but what was it trying to say? That his lover was going to try to kill him? He closed his eyes, and shuddered. The poppy had been a good sign. The choking and the dress had nearly made him run for his life. His instincts were telling him to be careful, to be watchful, and so he decided this was what he would do. He would just try to enjoy the day, for Gretchel's sake, and watch her as closely as he could. Sometimes you have to sacrifice your happiness and just survive.

A distraction was welcome when Blake, who had played with Eli's guitar so many years ago at Gretchel's nineteenth birthday party, wanted to play for everyone. Eli was touched when Blake explained he fell in love with guitar that day, and fervently played ever since.

Eli retrieved two of his guitars, and let Blake play the Martin that Gretchel had decorated with crazy psychedelic flora while living at the House on Pringle. They sat around the bon fire that was burning bright, and strummed a few Stevie Ray Vaughn songs together, while Graham retrieved his custom-made drum rental and tapped at it with rhythmic precision. It had been way too long since Eli had played guitar. It was therapeutic, and settled him, though his eyes rarely left Gretchel's sight.

She was wandering around the yard visiting with Stephen, Teddy and his mother, Marie. Gretchel would flitter around the farmhands and flirt. Eli watched their reactions as she walked away. They shook their heads, licked their lips, and blew out wistful sighs. The affect she had on men was pathetically obvious. He was proud to say she was his mate, but he couldn't help but feel slighted by her shameless actions. He'd never seen her behave in such a way, though he knew she was capable. His heart was aching with an unpleasant case of the jellies.

Eli watched as Graham abandoned the drum to help Gretchel start the May Pole. He watched her take pictures of Miss Poni, Ella, Marcus, Blake and Brody, but always refusing to have her own picture taken with the family.

He then watched her go into the barn, and come back out with her bow and arrow. Diana was quick to join the shooting competition. She was also an archer, who had once competed at a collegiate level. Eli was thankful that she and Gretchel had a common factor with which to bond. At least he hoped they would bond. He was pleased his mother had found something to do, rather than pester Gretchel about her past or the poppy.

And the men certainly seemed to be enjoying the show. Eli was well aware they were gathered to watch the redheaded goddess in action, and not the sharp-bobbed tyrant. Eli put his uneasiness aside and watched Gretchel too. She was a site to behold. Not only was she skilled as a dangerously, powerful femme fatale, but she could also be lethal as a bowman. *Lethal.* Eli shuddered.

He watched Gretchel tease Blake and tried to talk him into a handfasting ceremony with his girlfriend, Hannah. He watched her watching his father as Graham flirted with Marie. Eli could see jealously in Gretchel's eyes; the feeling was contagious. With that, Eli decided he was done watching Gretchel, and he went to her instead.

She was sitting by herself, as far away from the fire as possible. Eli sat next to her, and gently took her hand.

"How you feeling?"

"I'm fine... Scratch that. I'm good. I'm having a

lovely time. It's just what I needed. Everyone I love is here, except my kids, of course," she smiled haphazardly.

Eli tightened the grip on her hand, and they watched merry revelry around the bon fire. It was getting very drunk out.

"So, it's Beltannnnne," Eli said, exaggerating the word and bouncing her hand up and down on the arm of the chair.

"Beltannnnne," Gretchel echoed in the same humorous tone.

Eli shot her a sideways grin. "Have you ever celebrated the intimate side of Beltane, Gretchel?"

She chuckled. "Yes, I have. Troy never allowed me to attend the festivities at Snyder Farms, but early in my marriage I celebrated Beltane intimately with an old family friend, and naturally, being the addict I am, once wasn't enough for me and we continued celebrating for way too long."

The old family friend, Eli cringed. "Is this the family friend who was your hunting partner?"

"Devon? Oh no, no, no. I'm fairly certain I finished my business with him. This old family friend–the one I celebrated Beltane with–well he and I still have unfinished business. It may never be settled."

This was not welcome news for Eli.

"What is that supposed to mean?" he asked, and as he did, he suddenly remembered a face. It was the man who he had drank tequila shots with at a downtown Irvine bar the night Ame had wrecked her car. The man claimed to have been with Gretchel. He claimed to have been involved in the truck accident. He needed to know who this punk was.

"It doesn't mean what you think. I don't plan to celebrate Beltane with him this year."

"Mighty nice of you," Eli mumbled under his breath. "So you cheated on Troy with this family friend. Did Troy ever find out? And doesn't that cancel out Troy cheating on you with Michelle?"

"No, he didn't find out, and for the record Troy cheated on me all the time! It was a completely dysfunctional marriage, which I thought I had conveyed to you already. I didn't give a fuck if Troy cheated or not, that was never the point, it was *who* he cheated on me *with* the last three years of his life that was the problem. I deserved what I got Eli, in more ways than one. There is no doubt about that, but that doesn't make it hurt any less. My feud with Michelle Brown goes back many years. I may have been the kerosene that kept that fire going, but she is the one that struck the match to begin with. We betrayed each other in the worst possible ways. Friends don't do that to each other. That makes her my adversary.

"Troy worked for her father, and we were neighbors. We were so intertwined with each other's lives that it almost seemed like a cruel joke. Imagine having to play nice for almost two decades with the person you loathe the most. She ruined my life, and she's still proud of it. Given the chance, she'd ruin it again." Gretchel steamed, and watched Eli's intrigued reaction. "Are you trying to get information out of me like I specifically asked you not to do, or are you just jealous? I never took you for the jealous type, Eli. Do you see a ring on this finger? We're not married."

"Would you like to be?" he asked coldly.

She softened, and regretted her outburst. She touched his cheek tenderly. "Of course I would like to be. Nothing would make me happier. Someday. Someday when I'm much saner and can consider myself worthy of being your wife."

"Sanity and marriage are both overrated," Graham interrupted. He grabbed Gretchel's hand and pulled her up. "I have an overwhelming urge to dance with you, Kittycat."

"Well keep your urges under control," Eli spat. "She doesn't dance anyway."

Gretchel shot Eli a dirty look. "I can speak for myself, thank you very much." She looked back to Graham. "No, thanks Mr. Duncan."

"It's just a dance, Honeylove. You sway your hips and move your feet with the rhythm. We did it last night. Remember?" he said.

Much to Eli's dismay, she allowed Graham to lead her away.

Eli sat back in his chair and watched them whirl around the yard. The familiarity of the scene jogged a memory. It was his reoccurring dream: Gretchel dancing in the firelight. His jealousy mimicked the flames of the bon fire.

Eli watched the other dancers. Marcus danced with Cindy, Ella danced with Thomas, Stephen danced with Teddy, and the farmhands all had a girl on his arm. One was even dancing with Miss Poni. Everyone had a partner. Even Blake and Brody sat by the stereo equipment, canoodling with their respective girlfriends.

Eli was envious. He felt a presence. He looked up to

see his mother with her shirt untucked, high heels off and a half empty bottle of wine in her hand.

"Mother, you're shitfaced!"

"Maybe so, maybe no. Danss with me Elliot. Mama wansa danss."

Face palm.

CHAPTER THIRTEEN
Irvine, 2010s

The crowd had grown since the early hours of dinner. It was a buoyant and gracious bunch. It reminded Miss Poni of days long gone. She thought there might never be another Beltane extravaganza in her lifetime after the truck accident, and she was most grateful to be proven wrong.

She sat by the bon fire. A small floral quilt that Gretchel had made for her years before lay over her lap. Miss Poni could sense she was being watched. She saw Diana in a merry-addled state stumbling her way. She carefully maneuvered her way across the yard, and fell into a chair.

Miss Poni smiled wickedly. "You are the most persistent woman I've ever met, Diana Stewart. I admire you for that."

Diana was taken aback. "You... Admire me?"

"Just a smidgen. I know what you have to gain from your time at Snyder Farms. I think it is more selfless than you realize. *You* think you are going to use this experience to prove your archetypal theories, and you think you are responsible for solving a mystery, but I know there is more to it than that."

Diana was befuddled. "You follow my work?"

A familiar crease crinkled in Miss Poni's brow. "I follow lots of things. If you're patient I may tell you another story soon. Just don't push Baby Girl. She pushes back."

Another story! Diana was ecstatic. But she needed Gretchel to start talking too. "I'm not scared of your granddaughter, Miss Poni."

Miss Poni patted Diana's leg. "You should be, you drunken ol' bitch! She's possessed. What experience do you have with supernatural ghosts, Diana? What do you know about calming a specter intent on destroying your direct family line? Ame is lucky to be living. Zachary is a true miracle. The one who haunts Baby Girl will stop at nothing to destroy anyone who will keep this family line going. That one is Ame. It is no mistake that Zach was drawn toward Chicago. That boy, though he's a rotten apple, is still intuitively sound. He has gifts just like Marcus, and his cousins. He knew, though not specifically, that he needed to get away from his mother and this farm. He was right. He wouldn't survive had he stayed. He's weaker than Ame, and wouldn't make it through the quest, which we soon embark. He is safe where he is now. He will come back after the Solstice. That is if his mother survives."

Diana was beside herself, and she was now cursing all the wine she'd consumed. Then she considered the possibility that Miss Poni was doing this on purpose. *Oh! She's a sharp old bird.* "First off, I'm not drunk, so let's address the danger you are insinuating."

"Gretchel *is* dangerous. Any fool can see that."

Diana frowned, and completely lost her train of thought. She gave up and returned to the rest of Miss Poni's comments. "As for your question on what experience I have with supernatural ghosts, don't forget I met the crone and Carlin."

The firelight shone bright on Miss Poni's face. It reflected a shimmering half-smile. "Carlin, my mother. She's here tonight, Diana. I can feel her watching us from the lake. This jovial gathering reminds me of the days when I was a child, and more so of when I was a young married woman. We'll get to that later. My mother would have loved this party. I can feel her blessing. Gretchel did us well."

Diana looked out over the party. It *was* a marvelous event. "She did indeed. Tell me Miss Poni, does Gretchel plan to throw a party for the Summer Solstice?"

Miss Poni cackled. "You think you're clever. I'm surprised you've caught on in your drunken stupor."

"Miss Poni, please answer the question. This could be very important information."

The old woman turned serious. "Oh, it *is* important information; of that you can be sure. There will be no party, but there will be a gathering, the most important gathering this family has ever had. Now if you will excuse me, Ms. Stewart, before I retire for the night I'd like to take a walk by the lake and visit with my mother."

Stonewalled again. Diana glanced at the lake, and noticed tiki torches lit up around the perimeter of the island. She looked back to Miss Poni's chair and the woman was gone, her quilt folded in the seat. Diana looked back to the lake that was at least one hundred yards away, and saw a figure hobbling along the island fence. "What the…" Diana started. She decided she had just witnessed an extraordinary act of magic or she was very drunk. It was most likely both.

∞

The energy was becoming rather rambunctious after more of Marcus's friends and members of the farming community joined the party. As much as Eli was all for getting a little loopy and stupid, he just wasn't in the mood, nor would he have drank in front of Gretchel. It was a simple consideration, and he would teetotal for the rest of his life if that's what it meant to be with her.

He watched her seductively flutter from person to person. The beer and wine flowed freely, and he thought he saw his father with a bottle of Absinthe. *Figures.* Eli took precaution to be sure Gretchel's chalice of iced tea was always full. He drank from her cup when she wasn't watching just to be sure she was staying clean. He was relieved she was handling the social pressures of the revels with such ease.

It was late when she sat down with one of the farmhand's children, while the parents danced. Graham and Eli both observed Gretchel as she cuddled the infant. It was a tender moment. She held him close, snuggling the baby between her shoulder and neck. Eli couldn't help but let his mind wander. He couldn't help fantasizing about it being Ame.

I should have seen this. I should have been there. It should have been me bringing my wife and baby home from the hospital, me helping out, me cherishing my daughter, me spoiling her, me loving her mother. It should have been me, he thought over and over again until a hand on his shoulder broke the egoic chant.

Graham had noticed his son's stare and troubled forehead. "Stay in the moment, Elliot," he whispered.

Gretchel looked up from her doting. "Would you like to hold him?"

Eli carefully took the baby, and cradled him in his arms. He was so tiny, so new, so breakable and innocent. Gretchel looked on lovingly. "You're pretty good at that, Hermes."

"I've been told that before. I remember when my best friend Andy's daughter was born. I held her for hours that first week. I was in love. She was a very sweet baby; calm and precious," he kissed the infant's tiny head, and then looked back at Gretchel. "What was Ame like as a baby?"

"She was a miserable little beast."

Eli and Graham were both startled by her answer.

Gretchel laughed. "She had colic, and I swear she was part Banshee by the way she screamed. She drove Troy up a wall," Gretchel smiled, and took the baby back. Graham chuckled madly.

I would have calmed her down. I would have found a way to soothe her. I would have been patient. I would have loved her like she should have been loved. She would have been fine had Troy not beat her mother while she was in the womb, Eli obsessed.

Graham cleared his throat. Eli took the hint. His expression was giving it all away. He never did have a decent poker face.

Gretchel's phone went off in her lap. "Would you grab that?" she asked swathing the child in blankets. Eli leaned in, kissed the baby on the head once more, and then snuck a peck at Gretchel's smiling lips. He felt around her lower region, teasing her until he finally located the phone. "It's a text. Probably Ame. Just open it," she said and rocked the baby.

"It's not Ame's number... it says *Merry Beltane Baby Girl. I need 2 talk 2 U ASAP*."

Gretchel's nostrils flared, she cuddled the baby with her right arm, and grabbed the phone with her left.

"Old friend of the family?" Eli asked sarcastically.

"And all around pain in the ass," she replied, then got up and walked away.

∞

Graham was buzzing quite happily when he noticed a familiar face staring at him from across the party. He gasped. It had been years since he'd seen this dazzling creature. She was absolutely beautiful, not as beautiful as Gretchel, but attractive in a whole different way, a sophisticated, ravishing, otherworldly way. Graham had missed her sorely.

The face nodded in recognition, and spread her delicate, translucent wings. They were massive, and glowed luminous against the flames of the Beltane fire. These moments never ceased to leave the great, elusive Graham Duncan in a state of mysterious awe. It reminded him as his childhood, when he'd first met her at the House on Pringle.

Within the blink of an eye the woman occupied the

chair Eli had been wallowing in only moments before. "Claire!" Graham cried.

"My darling, Graham," Claire cooed, hugging him tightly.

Graham had no qualms about visiting with this beautiful fairy in public. He didn't know if anyone else could see her, and he couldn't quite believe he was seeing her again either. Was it the Absinthe that was known for encouraging fairy sightings? Was it Beltane's veil being lifted? He didn't know. He didn't care. He was just happy to be seeing her again.

"Oh Claire, you're exquisite as always. Has ten years or more past since we've last communed?"

With her wings now tucked in, he noticed her gown that was a flowing silk, with patterns of magnolia and patches of blue skies. She had no imperfections, and looked the same as the day they'd first met.

"It has been too many years, and I knew one day we would meet again under the watchful eye of the Goddess."

They both grinned at the moon, and closed their eyes in silent blessing.

"What brings you to Irvine of all places?"

"I'm bound by code. Graham, do you remember when we met?"

"Of course!" He had been five-years-old, and she appeared to him as he played lazily near the statue of Pan is his mother's gardens.

"A day will come, the Solstice in fact, when you will need to remember the details of our meeting with great clarity. It will guide you through the mayhem."

Graham became quite serious. "Then there's trouble

ahead?"

"There is an opportunity for redemption for us *all*."

"Ever the optimist. I adore you, Claire."

"And I you." She smiled and touched his cheek.

Graham felt something materialize in his hand. He took a gander to find a small pouch. "What's this?"

"A bit of temporary paralysis magic. Keep it close," she said, her tone serious.

"More trouble?"

"I'm bound by code. Peace be with you." A sly smirk grew on her perfect face as she gazed at an approaching visitor. She sighed. Another source of trouble was already present.

Diana stumbled toward them spouting irrationals. "Hey. Hey, you have fairy wings. I saw them open and close," she shouted.

Before Graham could keep his wife from scaring Claire, the fairy had gone and Ella stood behind him. Graham was thoroughly confused.

"Ella, you're a fairy," Diana said, she looked contemplative, as she rummaged through her mental folklore filing cabinet. "You were born on Beltane, and you have wings I saw them Ella."

Gretchel and Eli had joined the conversation. "Her real name's Elphame, so maybe she is a fairy," Gretchel laughed. She thought it refreshing to see Diana so out of control.

"Yes! Elphame is the fairy queen. The Queen of May Day!" Diana rattled, barely coherent.

Teddy sidled up to Ella. "Silence her," he whispered.

"If my magic worked on the wicked woman, I

would have silenced her days ago," Ella whispered back.

Gretchel growled at the drunken spectacle. She remembered the days when she was the obnoxious one. It conjured mixed feelings of gratitude and annoyance. She looked to Eli. "Get her out of her."

"The fairy queen! She's the goddamn fairy queen, Graham!" Diana continued to shout. "I need my tablet! Eli, go fetch my tablet."

Eli looked at his watch. It was close to midnight. He quickly decided his parents would stay at the cottage in Zach's old dormer. It was rather hard for him to tell if his father was really messed up or just normal. It was always hard to tell. Diana, however, was crocked.

"Come on, Mother. Time for bed."

"Get me my tablet. I need to record this fairy sighting."

"It's inside, Mom. How about we go get it?" Eli said.

Graham roared with laughter. "Now you're learning, buddy boy!"

"I'm ready to go to sleep too. How about you?" Gretchel asked, after Diana had been dumped into bed.

Eli agreed.

They undressed in silence. "You were quiet today, Eli. You weren't your sweet, charming self," Gretchel started. "Please don't worry about me."

"I was tired and my stomach's been queasy."

Gretchel climbed in bed as text notification went off on her phone.

"Didn't Ame just text you?" Eli asked.

"Yeah."

She opened the new text, read the message. Eli pulled the covers up, and turned off the lamp. After a few moments, he turned to see Gretchel still staring at the phone. The glow of the screen lit up a face full of distress.

"What's wrong?" he asked.

She shook her head. "Nothing. It's fine." She put the phone on her nightstand, grabbed her rag doll and settled on her side.

Eli felt like he might throw up again. Something was wrong. He stared at the ceiling and listened to the party until he felt Gretchel jerk. He knew she had drifted. He grabbed her phone and read the text.

Talked to Zach, said he's staying the summer in Chicago. CALL ME!

The old family friend.

∞

Eli tried not to toss and turn, and he dare not close his eyes. The last time Gretchel had a severe psychotic break it involved her son. He glanced at her sleeping so soundly, and wondered how someone so precious and lovely could be so formidable.

He listened to the sounds of the party. It was 3am before it finally died down. The jollification had kept him awake. About the time the last car pulled out of the drive, was when he drifted into a deep sleep.

Gretchel was entertaining a reoccurring nightmare. She was wearing the dress she'd created for the Solstice, and it was hot outside. Very, very hot.

Ah bloody hell! an ancestor hollered. *Ye couldn't pay me a bag o' gold' coins to stay in this dream!*

Ye bloody radge girl! Bloody radge!

Shoot the craw! Shoot the craw!

The ancestors had been congregated around Gretchel in the Wicked Garden, and in a panic they ran toward the lake and dove in.

"Please stay, I need you! Carlin! Bridget! Help me!" she screamed to the only ancestors whose name she knew. She saw what had frightened them. A black mare was walking toward her, his gate full of purpose.

"No!" Gretchel screamed, and realized for the millionth time that no one in dreamland responded to her pleas.

Her attempts at running failed. She fell to the cold earth. Diana was atop the mare holding Troy's fraternity paddle. She made to strike, but Gretchel pulled herself away and cowered under the large oak tree for protection. She watched in horror as the mare turned from black to white. "Goddess be with me," she whispered.

And then she saw that Diana was no longer the rider. It was Eli! The horse continued to change shades, and Eli held the paddle firmly.

"No!" she screamed. "Eli, you mean me no harm! You're good to me!"

Then she felt herself being pulled with unimaginable strength. Her fingers barely grasped the rough bark of the oak's trunk. The pull lifted her body. There was an opening in the ground. It was a spinning, fiery vortex. "No! I can't go there yet! I can't!" she screamed.

"She's waiting for you," a voice whispered. It came from Gretchel's rag doll. It appeared in the broken passenger side window of the truck, unaffected by the unnatural pull. The doll slowly morphed into Holly.

Gretchel's heart beat madly. She couldn't wrap her head around the chaos. Her niece was dressed in a familiar pair of pajamas.

"Oh gods no," Gretchel whispered in horror. She knew those pajamas all too well. They were light pink and cotton. She remembered how they'd been covered with blood and...

"She's waiting for you," Holly said.

Gretchel couldn't breathe as she watched Holly morphed into another young girl. "No!" she screamed. She held tight to the tree and the dream, as she witnessed the girl get sucked into the flaming abyss.

The twentieth descendant.
The sacrifice.

Gretchel awoke with a jerk.

She saw Eli sound asleep, and for that she was grateful. She used the bed sheet to wipe her sweaty brow, and when the sheet lowered the Woman in Wool was staring at her from the doorway.

Gretchel drew her hands up to her mouth in an effort to muffle her sobs. It was sheer terror seeing the Woman in Wool as a fully realized ghost again.

"Ye donnae have to go there. Ye can stop all the

madness."

"How?" Gretchel whimpered.

"Kill the psychopomps."

CHAPTER FOURTEEN
Irvine, 2010s

A door slammed in Graham's dream. Startled awake, he sat straight up, and scanned the dark room. He let out a routine sigh of relief. Once again, the feds had not come to steal him away from his son. The fear was constant and deep-rooted. He must never be separated from his boy. The messenger would need him someday. Graham was thankful there was no law enforcement banging down his door, but still he felt danger. Something sinister was lurking at Snyder Farms.

He pulled on wrinkled suit pants, and slipped on his Birkenstocks. Like a thief in the night, he slipped down the stairs. Through the sunroom window he saw a shadow creeping toward the barn. "Something's lit the dynamite," he whispered, and then surreptitiously disappeared into the dark morning.

Ame was furious as Peyton tried to hold her hand in the back seat of the limo. She'd traded her dress for a concert t-shirt, jeans and tennis shoes, but was still uncomfortable; though it surely had little to do with the clothes she wore. Prom had been prom. She would have much rather been at the Beltane celebration watching over the ones she loved. Someone needed to protect them from her mother and the Woman in Wool. Ame sometimes felt she was only sane one capable of offering that protection. The recent secret meetings she'd had with Miss Poni were sharpening her skills and aiding in her confidence.

She tried to get magic and her mother off her mind for the moment. She reflected back on prom. Of course her friends had all goggled over Peyton. *Perfect*, was the word Ame kept hearing. *If he's perfect then they are lousy judges of character*, she thought. She sulked. He was close to perfect for her. But was there a perfect man? Or would he turn out just like Troy. How would she be able to tell?

Peyton had said those three magic words at the wild post-prom party, and Ame hadn't answered him. He caught her off guard, and that's why she was uncomfortable. She didn't relish the idea of her guard being down at all.

"What's wrong?" Peyton asked, with remnants of warm, stale beer on his breath.

Ame cringed. She shook her head, and stared out the window. She hated this. She hated being ambivalent. She was a girl who knew what she wanted, and she had thought she wanted Peyton. He of course was kinder, smarter and cuter than any of the other boys she'd dated. He'd taken her virginity.... No, no, no. She'd *given* him her virginity, and while he treated the handful of times they'd had sex with the utmost dignity and respect, she was still scared.

What the hell am I scared of? Nothing scares me! She took that back too... Gretchel scared her. Her mom's insanity terrified her, and she was not naïve enough to believe it was just possession. The truck accident had screwed Gretchel up good. Ame pitied her in a way, but she was also determined to do whatever it took to not be like her mother, but what in the hell did she want to be like? Eli-with-an-I was slacking on his promise. And that reminded her that she needed to speak to him ASAP about Holly and the psychopomps.

She feigned annoyance, and stole a glance at Peyton. She adored him. Maybe that's why she was scared. He made her feel like she had no control. There were moments when he inspired great bouts of strength in her, but then there were moments when he inspired tenderness and submission. It made her skin crawl. *No. No. No! I don't care how good it feels, I will not let the walls down! I was born a giant, and I will not be shrunken down to size by anyone.*

∞

It was a difficult night sleep for almost everyone at Snyder Farms, and Diana was not to be excluded. The sound of rubber against gravel awoke her from a hazy slumber. She heard the vexatious beginnings of an adolescent argument. She sat up quickly, and instantly regretted the move. She clutched her head as if trying to hold in the brain that had turned to lush mush during her evening of overindulgence. With great effort, she finally pulled herself to the dormer window. Ame was home, and throwing a fit. Diana couldn't help but pry; it was her nature. She cracked the window and listened.

"What's the matter now?" Peyton fumed.

"You! You are what's the matter."

"What did I do this time?"

"You said that you loved me," Ame told the boy.

Peyton raised his hand, and Ame instinctively flinched, gripped her fist and drew her arm back preparing for battle. Peyton softly brought his hand down on her shoulder. "Jesus Christ! I'm not going to hit you, Ame. I can't even touch you these days without incident. Not every man is an asshole like your dad... I mean Troy. Please believe me when I say you're safe with me."

My god, Troy must have tortured her, Diana thought, wiping the sleep from her eyes.

"I'm too young to commit myself to one person," Ame said through hot tears.

"I just want to have fun with you. Isn't that what love is about? I'm not asking you to marry me yet. I'm just telling you how I feel," Peyton tried.

Ame brushed his hand off her shoulder. "I don't need you up in my grill all the time. Stop touching me, and stop acting like you can control me."

"I didn't do anything! I kissed your ass all day, I went to the stupid prom, I spent money for you and I did everything you wanted me to do. What is your problem?"

"You're my problem! You're a man, and that automatically makes you my problem."

"Are you gay?"

"You're a fucking moron." Ame shook her head in

disbelief. "You just don't get it."

"What is there to get? Help me understand. Is it because of Troy? Is that why you're acting this way?"

Ame's eyes lit up with a whole new fury. She thought she might coldcock Peyton just for the minor offense of being so dense. "Don't ever mention his name again! *Ever!* You need to leave. You need to go before I rip your fucking head off!"

And here comes the rage, Diana thought.

Peyton held his hands up in surrender. "Fine. I'll leave... again... but I'll be back... again. You love me Ame Duncan. I know you do, and I have time to wait."

Ame was momentarily paralyzed by the sound of her true last name. By the time she could think this through Peyton was in his car backing out of the driveway.

"I don't need you!" she screamed. "I have a man already, and he doesn't talk back to me," she turned herself around and threw her arms in the air. "Why? Why won't you talk back to me! Why won't you show yourself! You stopped guiding me! Where are you?" she screamed into the open air.

Diana's eyes were as big as two chocolate coins. *The Horned God?* she wondered. *Oh I can't do this*. The hangover reached out its hand and bitch-slapped her silly.

∞

Graham waited in the shadows during Ame's temper tantrum, during which time a light turned on in the barn. Ame noticed the light, but was too caught up in her frenzy to find it out of the ordinary. She stomped into the house. *Good it's where she needs to be*, Graham thought.

The barn door was ajar, leaving just barely enough space for him to squeeze. He quickly sidled in, and concealed himself behind a mound of hay. Peaking around, he saw Gretchel. "Shitsticks," he whispered. He prayed for a miracle to save this woman from the atrocity she was about to commit.

∞

Ame raged into the house, waking Eli with the slam of the door.

He came running into the living room, pulling on a sweatshirt. Ame was already on her knees praying to the stag that hung above the mantel. "Why won't you show yourself to me?" she begged.

Eli hastily interrupted her prayer. "Where's your mom?"

"Eli! I have to talk to you about what Holly said in the Wicked Garden yesterday?"

"Your mom's gone. Have you seen her? Where is she?"

Ame had never seen Eli this distraught. She glanced at the time. "She's probably running like normal. Eli, I have to talk to you about what Holly said! Please quit worrying about my childish mother for a second, and listen to me!"

"I do listen to you, and I will again, but we have to find Gretchel first!" he bellowed.

Ame was silenced by his thunderous voice. "Look

Ame," he said in a state of panic, "I've got a bad feeling something's going to happen. Someone sent her a text last night saying Zach was staying the summer in Chicago, and I'm afraid it's set her off. We've got to find her."

Ame nervously rubbed the amethyst necklace between her fingers, and the answer became clear. "The barn," she whispered.

"What?"

"When I came in, the barn light was on. It just dawned on me," she said. Suddenly they heard barking coming from the dormers. "She locked up Suzy-Q?"

"Because Suzy-Q barks when something's amiss. Leave her there. Let's go!" Eli yelled. The nausea of the prior day's worries returned. His stomach was doing kamikaze flip-flops as he and his daughter went chasing after danger.

Epona was frighteningly still at the far end of the barn. Gretchel stood broadside to the mare, her finely tuned Bear Archery bow drawn with a broadhead tipped-carbon arrow resting in the knock. It was deadly to say the least.

She suddenly released her draw, and lowered the bow.

"I can't do it!" she sobbed.

Graham watched nervously from his post.

"Kill her!" screamed the Woman in Wool.

"Why?" she questioned.

"'Cause they'll have us relive it all again. We're not fit fer forgivn'."

"You're right about that. You were always right

about that," Gretchel cried.

She retracted her arm again, and holding her sight on target, she was ready to trigger the string release.

At that moment Ame and Eli slipped into the barn, and the creaking sound of the door distracted Gretchel from her mission.

"Get down," Graham frantically whispered.

"Aye! Now there's an even finer target!" the Woman in Wool decided.

Gretchel turned, saw the psychopomps and deliberately let the arrow loose. It bolted across the barn, and hit the door with a thud–directly between Eli and Ame, within inches of either's forehead.

Ame fell back, and slipped to the ground in complete shock. Eli's stomach had reached its limit, and the vomit came rushing up all over the barn floor.

"I'm sorry! I'm sorry! I'm so sorry!" Gretchel shrieked. She dropped the bow and ran toward them.

Graham jolted out, tackling her. "This isn't how I pictured our first wrestling match, Kittycat," he said.

He held her down, though she fought to be freed. "I'm sorry! I'm sorry!" she screamed. "I didn't want to do this! I'm sorry! Please don't take me away!"

"Honeylove, I'm sorry too, but you're going have to take one for the team this time," Graham said. He held her down with one arm and his knee. Reaching in his pocket he found the pouch Claire had provided. A fine powder, citrusy and yellow spilled onto Gretchel's face. Within moments she was unconscious.

CHAPTER FIFTEEN

Irvine, 2010s

"What in the *fuck* was that?" Eli bellowed at the top of his lungs, when he was finally able to stop the dry heaves.

"It appears she wants us dead," Ame whispered, just barely able to catch her breath.

"Why does Gretchel want us dead?" Eli shouted.

"Not Mom. The voice. The Woman in Wool."

Graham paced the barn. Pacing was not his thing, but neither was forcing the most beautiful, dynamic woman he'd ever come across to lose consciousness. *It's an adventure, it's what you wanted, now deal with it,* he told himself.

"I have to tell Diana," he announced, perhaps more to convince himself.

Eli shook his head fiercely, the curls a riot of protest. "Absolutely not! She'll want her to be hospitalized."

"She almost killed you, Elliot!" Graham spat. "She needs to be hospitalized."

"You of all people know there's got to be another way to fix this without putting her back in the hospital. It'll destroy her. You've got to help me. You've got to help her."

"I have to tell your mother," Graham repeated.

Ame finally pulled herself off of the barn floor, and went to comfort Epona. "Take her away," she whispered.

"What?" Eli asked incredulously.

"You were going to St. Louis this week anyway. Go early. Take Mom away today. There are a million things there to keep her busy all week. She *needs* to get out. She's too cooped up in her mind here. The solitude of this cottage started as a good thing, but it's become a crutch. It's become too easy for the voice to reach her. You have to get her away, around society. Graham can tell Diana what's happened, but you'll already be gone. By the time you get back she can prove to Diana that she's regained some kind of grip on reality. And maybe by then we will have figured out some way to defeat this redheaded ghost that's trying to bury us."

Eli was suddenly very still. "Did you see the Woman in Wool commanding your mother?"

Ame's eyes were full of tears. "Yes, and she wants me dead."

Eli and Ame were like two very tall sprites fluttering around the bedroom packing suitcases. Eli thought his heart would pop out of his chest when he heard his mother's footsteps in the dormers. He finished throwing in his clothes, and then ran to the bathroom to grab toiletries.

Graham scurried into the bedroom, grabbed Eli's

messenger bag, and looked at Ame. "You didn't see anything," he said. She nodded indifferently, as she watched him slip a small, brown paper bag inside the tote.

Eli zipped into the living room where Gretchel was on the couch with her head in her hands. Eli knelt down to her. "It's going to be okay. I promise you," he said and kissed her hand. Gretchel had heard him say that many times before, and she was still waiting for it to be true.

"I have to help Mama pick strawberries this week," Gretchel whimpered.

Eli kissed her other hand. "It will get done, Baby Girl. I promise the farm will get by without you."

∞

By 6:30 they were on I-70 heading to St. Louis. Eli tapped the steering wheel nervously. He absentmindedly changed the radio channels. He tried not to let on that he was completely freaked out about the fact that Gretchel nearly murdered him again. It was not an easy task. They were both been very quiet. Eli felt compelled to discuss her about her son.

"Gretchel, please let me get my lawyers involved. We can have Zach back here in no time."

She was adamant. "No! He has to come back on his own volition or he will never forgive me. There's already enough reason for him to hate me without forcing this, and he'll know what that reason is soon enough. Drop it."

More secrets. Great! Eli swallowed his anger,

gripped the steering wheel and did everything he could to keep his mouth shut. Gretchel's phone sounded off multiple times with text message notifications. She would read them, and then stare out the window without answering.

At a gas station, Eli stayed in the car and grabbed her phone. It was not his normal code of conduct to disrespect a person's privacy, but considering Gretchel's sanity, he considered it a protection policy. He opened one of the texts, and dialed the number.

A man answered.

"It's about time you called, Gretchel. Now give me the damn address so I can go get Zach."

"Who the hell is this?" Eli roared. Silence. "Answer me, damn it!" Silence. "Have it your way, but I swear if you ever call this number again I will hunt you down and make you regret the day you set eyes on my future wife!"

"This is none of your business, man," a voice boomed back. "You don't understand what's going on."

"No shit? And, yes, it is my business, because your text last night sent Gretchel over the edge this morning!"

"Is she okay?"

"Oh she's just lovely. Ame and I were just about smoked by one of her arrows, but other than that everything's just amazing!"

"I need that address."

"Go fuck yourself, and don't you dare text or call this number again unless you want a size thirteen up your ass."

Click.

BELTANE

∞

"She what?" squawked Diana, with hair all a-tangle and make-up smeared. The outrageous hangover was intensifying her already frightening demeanor. Graham and Ame looked at each other, grasping for a worthy excuse.

"It was a bit of a blur..."

"I don't remember the details..."

"She may have been practicing..."

"Yes, yes I think she was..."

"I thought her aim was much better..."

"She might to be losing her touch..."

"Quiet!" Diana barked at the pair. This did not fair well for the hangover she was nursing. Her temples pulsated like a nightclub speaker. She felt like scratching her own eyes out, they were so dry. And her patience was wearing as thin as the veil had been on Beltane.

With purpose, she marched up to Graham, and stuck a finger in his face. "If that giant hurts my son she'll have hell to pay."

In an instant Ame whirled her grandmother around, the bob swirling like a dancing skirt. She slammed Diana against the wall. "If you ever refer to my mother as a giant again, *you'll* have hell to pay you despicable little woman!" She glared at her grandmother with fierce gray eyes. For a second they both felt a mutual knowing: and it was *fear*. Ame let her go, and then stormed out the kitchen door.

Diana's mouth was agape. No one had ever laid hands on her in anger. Her eyes blazed ire at Graham who stood quiet and wide-eyed. "Thanks for the support asshole!"

"You get what you give, Diana. Why is that so difficult for people to understand?"

∞

Ame sought solace with her maternal grandmothers at the house on the hill. She had magic to learn anyway, and it was safer to keep her distance from Diana until she'd calmed down.

Graham spent the rest of the weekend helping Marcus and his boys clean up after the Beltane celebration, and exploring the countryside by four-wheeler. Diana reluctantly spent her weekend lying on the couch recovering from the rare evening of over-intoxication. She cursed herself for wasting a perfectly good opportunity to search the house for clues.

They were both relieved when Ame returned to the cottage Monday evening. Ame said hello to Graham upon entering the house. She ignored Diana and went straight up to her dormer. Diana could no longer handle the guilt. She snuck up the stairs, and knocked at the open door. Ame had just settled onto her bed, and opened her homework, when Diana appeared in the doorway. Ame sighed and waved her grandmother in.

Diana initially caught herself sneering at the unwelcoming teenager. She had to force herself to play nice. She looked around the spacious bedroom. The walls were covered in beautiful purple damask wallpaper, free of posters or the typical teenage decor. There was a small black vanity, which had plenty of beauty supplies, but not to the extent Diana thought she would see. Instead the bedroom was filled with a large black desk hosting stacks of notebooks, journals and a laptop. A quaint little book nook was filled with teal and mustard pillows and a chair covered in peacock feather print. Diana couldn't ignore the wall-to-wall black shelves that housed a large number of books, jarred herbs, magical supplies and more crystals than Diana had seen in one place.

Investigating the book titles, Diana saw all of Graham Duncan's works; she expected that. Ame also had the typical Pagan fictions and non-fictions including every Ellen Dugan book printed.

"Who is Ellen Dugan?" Diana asked.

Ame looked at her grandmother as if she were a Martian. "Aren't you Pagan?"

"I asked you a question young lady, and it is rude to answer with a question of your own," Diana snapped.

Ame's nose flared. "Ellen Dugan is the Garden Witch. She's one of my most trusted resources for modern magic and someone I very much look up to, unlike you."

Diana put her hands on her hips. She'd had just about enough of this girl. Ah, but it was her grandchild, and she'd come up to mend fences. "I apologize for calling your mother a giant." Diana raced through the apology as if the words burnt her throat.

"Apology accepted," Ame said, hoping Diana would get the hint and leave. She wanted some quiet. She was glad to be home from school, away from all the prom gossip about who shagged whom, and who got wasted and what they got wasted on. She had more important things to worry about, like if her mother was going to kill her upon returning to Irvine. But at least the rumors about her paternity and accident had become old news, and for that she was grateful.

She was home now after her physical therapy appointment and away from the theatrics of adolescence, but now she had to deal with Diana, who, with Graham, had volunteered to be her guardians for the week.

Diana bowed her head, and let go of her anger. "I know we haven't seen eye to eye since I've arrived, but perhaps we can start over. I would very much like it if we could," Diana said and sat down on the edge of Ame's bed. Diana glanced at the girl's long legs that stretched off the edge of the mattress.

"Quit staring. I know I'm tall, but have some common decency. Starting over sounds good to me, but only if you get at least three feet out of my bubble."

Diana continued her peacemaking attempts, and found a seat at Ame's desk. "You don't like anyone in your personal space. I understand."

"Don't. Don't you do it," Ame pointed. "That is not the way to start over. Don't start analyzing me like I know you've been doing to my mother since you've arrived. I'm sure you've got notebooks piled to the ceiling about her by now, but I'm not going to be one of those case studies. I'm a person, not a file. I am your granddaughter, not a client, not a patient, nor a pawn in your little vision quest. Treat me like you would a regular person or is this how you treat everyone?"

Diana bit her tongue. These redheaded witches were going to get the best of her yet, though part of this girl's cheeky boldness was probably given to her through herself or Graham, mix in Gretchel as a mother and you got one rather saucy princess who was prepared to take over the kingdom. Diana held her hands up in surrender.

"And no, I do not like anyone in my personal space. You are aware a man who I believed was my father abused me all my life. Let's not start getting coy now. He beat me on a regular basis when I was kid, of course when I got older it was a little harder because I was taller than him, and I'd grown strong because of his mistreatment. He used to call my mom *giant this* and *giant that*. My mom was usually the *giant whore* and I was the *giant whorelet*. That started when I was ten! On rare occasion he would beat my brother, but not long, because I would always intervene to save him. I watched Troy beat my mother ruthlessly for the most mundane of offenses. I watched him kill her spirit a little every day, until she was barely a wisp of a human being. I will never allow a man to do that to me, and I will never allow anyone to get away with using that *giant* word in a derogatory tone with my mother. Someone has to protect her."

Diana was feeling something odd…. Compassion? "But my dear who is going to protect *you* from *her*?"

Ame was speechless.

Big tears flowed down face without permission. She hid herself with a sweatshirt, but couldn't stop the sobs that came pouring out in full force. Diana went back to the bed. "Darling, may I comfort you?" she asked. Ame shook her head *yes*.

Diana wrapped her tiny arms around the huge body that was hunched over on the bed, red hair draping her figure.

"There's nothing wrong with being a large woman,

Ame. Goodness what I wouldn't give to be at least an inch taller," Diana lightly chuckled. "Darling, what that man did to you was horrendous. It was an abomination, but you survived and he did not. You lived through it, and are a stronger person now. I don't think in all my years that I have seen a spirit more driven and determined as yours. My parents would have been so proud of you. I'm proud of you."

Ame looked up red-eyed and still shaking from the sobs. "Thank you," she whispered.

Diana hugged her tightly. "By the by, I'd like to take a look at your mother's sketchpads, Eli says she's quite the artist, but this shorty can't reach them as they're on top of the bloody refrigerator. Would you mind getting them down for me?"

Ame smiled. "Sure, but I want you to do something for me."

"What is it, love? Anything."

"I want to visit Troy's grave site while my mom's gone, and I want you to go with me."

CHAPTER SIXTEEN
St. Louis, 2010s

Gretchel hadn't watched much television since she moving to the cottage. While in St. Louis, she made up for lost time. After showering, she threw on lounge clothes and collapsed on the bed without drying her hair. She zoned out for an HGTV marathon.

Eli barely spoke. He dozed off and on; though he tried his best to stay awake in order to keep an eye on the gorgeous chick with the screw loose, even if it meant learning everything there was to know about home and garden. He knew Gretchel was enjoying the programming, but personally he didn't need to know how to choose the perfect color for a nursery (though it would have been his dream come true to raise a baby with Gretchel) nor create a homemade piñata and he already knew how to tend to an herb garden–of the psychedelic variety.

He was cursing Hestia the goddess of all things hearth and homey by mid-afternoon. A cornucopia from room service did little to distract Gretchel from her cozy trance. Eli was desperately trying to be grateful for the rare moments of normalcy, but when a repeat of the same episode he'd just watched that morning came on in the evening he lie on his stomach and put the pillow over his head to muffle an embittered howl.

At ten o'clock that night, he sat in the corner of the room contemplating. Gretchel was sleeping. Her long red hair lay flat across his pillow. The hair was definitive of her personality, and she treated it as if it were another child. He was drawn to the bed to caress the precious mane as she slept.

He was glad she'd finally rested despite the homey torture of cable TV. All he wanted was for her to find peace and joy. All he wanted was to live harmoniously. All he wanted was a map to the labyrinth that was Gretchel. All he wanted was her sanity, but instead his own seemed to be quickly slipping away.

"What the hell is this?" Gretchel asked the next morning, finally breaking the stiff silence that was growing between them. She pulled several pieces of clothing out of her suitcase.

"What's the matter?"

"Ame packed me a bunch of crap, that's what's the matter. I can't wear this stuff out in public all week," she complained looking at a pile of cropped sweatpants and concert t-shirts.

Eli was floored by her self-centeredness.

"We were in a bit of a hurry Gretchel," he said curtly. He made a bow hunting motion to remind her why they'd left in a rush. "Look, we'll go shopping. You can get whatever you want. Buy out the whole damn store for all I care. Let's just get the hell out of this hotel room before I rip the bloody hair right out of my scalp. You wouldn't want that now would you? All my curls in a pile on the floor?" he asked.

She looked at him astounded. "Oh no, Hermes. The curls must stay."

∞

Two hours into the shopping spree, Eli was begging to go back to the hotel for more home and garden television. Sometimes men can't win.

"You can go do something else, I'm not going to run off and kill somebody!" Gretchel shouted in the middle of a chic boutique. Eli felt a dozen pair of mascaraed eyes on him. He kindly handed the whip back to Gretchel, and didn't utter a whine nor complaint the rest of the afternoon.

Although he'd brought plenty of clothes, including his Armani suit for the surprise evening later in the week, he still decided to do a little shopping. It wasn't a difficult task. Cargo shorts: olive, brown, khaki, and various plaids. Done. T-shirts. Polo Shirts. Done. Jeans and khaki pants. Done. Boxers. Check. Couple of pair of shoes. Sack 'em up. Cardinal baseball cap. Thank you, come again. *Don't hold your breath pal.* There was a reason he had a personal shopper in Oregon to tend to his high fashion needs. Shopping was not a sport he relished.

He had strayed from Gretchel's side only once, when a knotted snake bracelet caught his eye. It would be beautiful on Gretchel. It was odd how some things are just meant to belong to certain people. He told her to go ahead to the handbag section and he'd catch up.

After dropping ten grand on the bracelet, he found Gretchel standing very still in front of a display. Eli observed with deliberation. He checked his watch. Eleven minutes had passed and she hadn't moved.

A chill ran through him. He approached loudly, to rouse her without shock.

"Hi Hermes," she said softly.

He looked over her shoulder at the object of her affection, and there sat a small handbag. It was shaped like a trapezoid, with a tiny blue handle. It was decorated with a whimsical scene. The top of the purse mimicked the clouds in the sky, and an ivory white front depicted a man riding a wild pig after a redheaded woman on a 12-point buck. The man held a bag of some kind. It looked as if he were chasing her down, as if she had forgotten. Eli felt like he was having déjà vu, but it wasn't. It was something altogether different. This hadn't happened yet, but it was going to. He shook out his wild curls. Was it a psychic moment? Or intuition? Or was it just plain get-me-the-fuck-out-of-this-boutique crazy? He didn't know. He didn't care. The purse was going with them.

"Get it," he said to her.

"Hmmm?" she asked, awakening slowly from her daze. "No. It's too expensive. Beautiful though isn't it?" she asked rhetorically and simply walked away.

Eli motioned for a clerk, who quickly wrapped up the handbag and checked him out as Gretchel browsed. He didn't even know what damn store they were in, until he looked down at the orange bag. *Hermes* was printed in small letters. The messenger.

BELTANE

∞

The St. Louis Cardinals were traveling that week. Damn the luck. Gretchel wanted to take Eli to Busch Stadium for a game. Eli really wanted to see a game, and to be around a little testosterone. It was not to be. *Another time*, she promised.

Instead, on Tuesday Gretchel decided they would visit the Missouri Botanical Gardens. It was her wheelhouse. Gretchel was at home amid the greenery and flora. Spring had truly sprung, and they both felt the magic of Persephone, the goddess of spring, within the illustrious acreage. Eli snapped photo after photo. The only thing that could compare to seeing Gretchel face-to-face was seeing her through the lens of a camera. His muse. His Aphrodite.

Later, they dined on The Hill, visited the St. Louis Arch, the Museum of Westward Expansion that was housed below, walked the riverfront, strolled around LaClede's Landing at dusk, and then collapsed in their hotel bed. Gretchel's body pointed in the opposite direction of Eli's much to his dismay. It had been nearly a week since they'd been intimate. He became irritable at the thought.

Wednesday they visited the St. Louis Art Museum, where Gretchel found herself in another kind of bliss. She was captivated by much of the artwork, and completely mesmerized by Van Gogh's *Stairway at Auvers*.

"You know," she said after a long, beautiful silence. "I already knew I had artistic ability before I saw my first Van Gogh. I knew art was my gift even as a little girl, but I never really threw myself into it until after I saw this painting. I understood him. I understood every mad, insane stroke the man painted. I felt it. I was always very empathetic like that. I could feel things even when they hurt and I didn't want to feel them. I knew when someone was in pain, when someone was anxious, worried, happy, exhilarated or depressed. I knew when they were blissed out and in love with life, but couldn't carry the full weight of their gift to the point that it drove them insane. And I knew how Van Gogh felt. Being as that he killed himself that may not be a good thing, eh?"

Eli pondered for a moment. "Baby Girl, I think if you can feel something that deeply it just means you're more alive than the rest of us."

That evening they dropped into bed again. Gretchel dressed in the same cotton capris and t-shirt even after he'd spent hundreds of dollars on lingerie during the shopping trip. She rolled over on her side as far away from him as she could get. He could tell she was feeling much better than she had, but she was still acting strange. Her life had been flipped upside down from the first day of the new-year. She had been through some very heavy, emotional turbulence. He tried to understand, and to a certain extent he did. Except for the sex. He was craving her.

On Thursday the manic tourist tour continued, with a trip to the St. Louis Zoo, more shopping and dining downtown. By the time they returned to the hotel, Eli was wiped out, backed up and pissed off.

Friday morning he showered in agitation. He

scrubbed roughly, and then wrapped a big white hotel towel around himself before standing in front of the mirror to shave. The tour of St. Louis was over. What a great town, but thank the gods it was over. The distractions had been welcome, but his underlying fear of the prophecy, the secrets, the insanity and her strange frigidness for three days, kept him from truly enjoying it like they should have. Perhaps the evening ahead would lift his spirits. He didn't know anymore. He didn't know anything, except that he really (really, really, really) wanted to get laid.

He finished shaving, and then bent over to rinse his face. When he brought himself up, a flash of red hair reflected in the mirror and startled him. Then he focused and saw that it was Gretchel in one of the new La Perla lingerie outfits.

She appeared unreal in the black lace and satin bustier. Garters attached to blush stockings and panties of the same design. As she walked toward him the short, blush chiffon kimono she wore flowed like butterfly wings. She was magnificent, and a merciful empath.

CHAPTER SEVENTEEN
Irvine, 2010s

Ame knelt before the cottage hearth. She was devout in her spiritual practice. She knew she was a bitter soul, and she knew one day she would be overcome with grace and be relieved of her resentments. For a moment thoughts of self-pity entered her mind... And then thoughts of self-hate came to pass. With prompt care, she chased them out and replaced them with a plea to the Goddess. "I am trying so hard to figure this out. I'm trying so hard to listen, and I know you've sent him to help us. I can feel him. Please give me a sign. Please, please allow the Horned God to show himself to me."

Graham walked in the front door, returning from a walk.

"Oh goodness. Pardon me love," he whispered, and backed out the door

She quickly–or as quickly as her still-injured body would allow–rose. "I'm done."

Graham bowed in acknowledgement, and entered

the cottage. He looked up at the buck and smiled. "Do you pray to the Horned God often, G-Bread?"

"Yes, and the Goddess, but I'm connected to the Horned God deeper. I've always felt his energy, even when I was a little kid, but I feel him very intensely right now. Is that normal? I know I'm quite aggressive. Seems I'm having some trouble letting go of my bitterness toward men."

Graham took her hand, and led her to the sofa.

"Do you understand the feminine and masculine energies?"

"Somewhat."

"Do you understand these energies have a certain ebb and flow to them?"

"Yes, but I have more of an ebb right now, and I'm having trouble flowing."

"Seems your mother has the same problem."

"Please don't tell me I've inherited her mental illness. I want to grow up to be anything but her," she said.

Graham laughed. *She'll rethink that statement someday*, he thought. "Do you want to be mentally ill?"

"No!"

"Then stop fighting it, and add some flow. Flowing's fun," he said, and went about his recent obsession of braiding and unbraiding his beard during conversation. Ame watched, captivated by the speed with which his nimble fingers worked. "Do you know anything about Jungian psychology?"

"Huh?" she redirected her attention from the beard to his bright aqua eyes. "Oh. Yes. A little. I understand that feminine energy is intuitive inner life and masculine is physical and manifest."

Graham nodded. "How about the anima and animus?"

"Come again?"

"We'll go to the metaphysical book store I saw in town and grab you some reading material."

"Oh! I used to work there. Claire was the best boss," Ame chimed. *Claire.* Suddenly she remembered seeing Claire at the cottage earlier that spring. She thought she did anyway. Maybe it was a dream. She wasn't sure about anything anymore. In fact, she thought maybe Miss Poni had charmed her memory rather strongly that night.

"Claire?" Graham asked.

"Yes. I'll introduce you when we shop."

"Indeed. I'd be very interested to meet your former employer," he said wondering. *No, surely not.*

"So you were waxing psychology…" Ame prodded.

They both had distraction issues it seemed.

"Oh yes. How can I explain this? Are you familiar with the character Mary in the book I wrote called *Sophia's Descent*?"

"That's my favorite book by you. Of course I know Mary."

"Well you are a lot like Mary right now."

"I'd rather be like Sophia."

"And I have no doubt you'll get there, G-Bread. No doubt. Now tell me more about this connection you have with Cernunnos, the Horned God–Celtic version of the Great God Pan."

She shrugged. "He loves me in a fatherly way, and he needs me. He's trying to call out to me. He's been calling to me all my life, and now that you and Diana are here I feel him more intensely than I ever have. I feel like I can almost hear him clearly, but it's always just a whisper in the back of my head that I can't make sense of, you know? Even right now in this very moment I feel like he's sitting right beside me, whispering in my ear. I feel like he needs my help, and I need his, as if there's something we have to do together. Something that we need to set straight, and I'm hoping that something is my mother."

Diana stood in the kitchen doorway nearly choking on a granola bar.

"Keep listening, G-Bread. Keep that mind open, and I'm sure the message will come through crystal clear. Perhaps someday soon."

"The prophecy?"

"Perhaps."

"Is there anything in the prophecy about the Horned God?" she inquired.

"I'm not at liberty to disclose information regarding the prophecy."

So there is, Ame thought.

"Will you go with us to the grave site? I think I'm ready, and I don't want to go with Mom."

"I would go to a barbecue in Hades with you, my fierce little warrior." He chuckled and kissed her freckled cheek.

"I'm hardly little. Do you think the devil likes potato salad?" Ame asked.

"Only if your mother makes it," Graham smiled.

"I'll be back in a few."

Diana zipped into the living room, and took Ame's seat.

Graham sang out before Diana could utter a word. "She's the twenty-first descendant, my love. You know that she is."

"No kidding," she growled.

"Maybe Holly's the twentieth," Graham pondered.

"No, no, no. I've already considered that. Yes she's from the bloodline, yes she's a few months older than Ame, but it's not her. The twentieth wouldn't have come from a male ancestor. Gretchel had another child, and when I find proof of that child I have a feeling everything is going to make more sense. Meanwhile, I've got to find out how Holly *is* involved. She was channeling in that garden, Graham. She knows things that she doesn't realize she knows. That poppy was a sign. The time is coming, and I still don't have my answers because Miss Poni and Ella are the most stubborn of witches. Not only that, I've got to figure out who the goddamned Horned God is. Ame can feel him, you heard her. How will this mysterious Horned God image point me toward an underworld? And what about the box? Where am I supposed to even begin looking for an ancient box, and what in the hell is inside that bloody thing that's so powerful?"

Graham watched her with squinted eyes. He'd lost interest at *No, no, no*. "Let's take Ame bowling."

"Goddamn it, Graham! Listen to me!"

"I am listening, and it's the same old thing I've heard over and over again. I want you to have your answers. I've wanted it for forty years."

"Well if your world is so malleable, Mr. Duncan,

why don't I have them yet? Why aren't you coming up with the answers for me if it's what you so desire? Huh? Why is the psychic clown, Graham Duncan, not *chewing on that?*"

"I'm going to shag you speechless, woman," he whispered.

Diana glared with eyes of steel. Then she continued her tirade. "Look at these." She threw three sketchpads in his lap.

He sifted through the first sketchpad. It was filled with self-portraits of a young teenage Gretchel, many of them shown with a mirror. "Narcissistic little thing isn't she?" Diana whispered.

Graham ignored his wife's comment, and moved on to the next pad. Poppies. The entire sketchpad was of poppies. The third pad contained various images: a large bon fire with a woman holding what appeared to be a silver Quaich. There was also a boat dock, field of poppies with an obvious clearing, a dark hole in the ground, a circular room containing doors with windows, a wolf, a snake, a stag, a black horse, a figure in a black hooded cape. Graham skimmed the images completely entranced. He finally came to the last sketch, which was what appeared to be the bottom of a lake with skeletons floating around a red mane of hair. Graham's skin came alive with goosebumps. The trip... He'd seen this image, only it was moving.

"Diana, I've seen this."

"What do you mean?"

"I saw the skeletons. When Elliot and I tripped a few months ago. He was laughing at them, giggling like he'd lost his marbles. Do we have any marbles? I haven't played marbles since Eli was a kid... I think I'll..."

"Goddamn it, Graham!"

"I've seen them, Diana. Oh! And Ame mentioned Sunday, though unintentionally, that she saw the Woman in Wool in the barn commanding Gretchel?"

"She's seen her?" Diana cried.

Graham nodded. "I think I've seen her too."

Diana face-palmed. Repetitively. "When did you see her?"

"I don't know. It's fuzzy."

"Why are you just now telling me these things?" she asked, clearly despondent, by her husband's short-term memory loss.

He shrugged. "The whole fuzzy thing?"

Diana's body shook. She wanted to choke him. She flat out wanted to rip him limb from limb. Graham took note of the twitch in her eye. "Darling, I may be a pacifist, but if you attack me I will bite the shit out of you."

"I'll protect you, G-Dizzle," Ame said.

Diana whipped her head around, and looked up...up...up to a towering figure. *How could a girl possibly be that tall? It's unnatural.*

"Ame, do you know what a Quaich is?" Diana asked.

"No clue, try again."

Diana sighed. "A Quaich is a cup that is traditionally used in wedding ceremonies. In Scotland its use can be dated back to at least the fifteenth century. It can also be called a loving cup. It has two handles..."

"Oh yeah. My mom's got one of those. It's on her dresser. It holds loose change."

Diana wasted no time jolting to Gretchel's bedroom. The dresser had Ame's prom dress laying across it, waiting to be taken to the dry cleaner. Diana gently removed the dress, revealing the silver cup underneath. She dumped the change on the dresser, turned the cup over and gasped.

"Whoa! What are you doing? That doesn't belong to you," Ame said as Diana returned to the living room with the cup. She couldn't believe her grandmother's audacity.

Diana smiled broadly. She did not give one iota that the cup did not belong to her. It was to whom it belonged to *before* that was important.

"Ame... This cup is a relic." She turned the cup over. On the bottom was an inscription: *Reid and Mage. Infinitely yours.*

"This cup belonged to the surviving Solstice Twin who is otherwise known as the Woman in Wool! This cup is hundreds of years old!"

Diana was beside herself with glee. She took picture after picture, and then returned the cup to Gretchel's bedroom, upon Ame's insistence. The two were getting along, yes, but Diana's boldness was no match for Ame's call of duty to protect her mother and her property.

"Any other mysteries I can help you solve, Diana Boss?" Ame waited for someone to laugh. She heard crickets. "Instead of Diana Ross? Get it?" Ame tried to explain.

"That's a good one G-Bread," Graham finally giggled.

"Meh. It sucked. I'm slacking in the joke

department. Too much stress."

Diana contemplating the new information she'd rendered.

"Ame, darling, your father told me you had your first experience with psychedelic mushrooms. He told me it was trying for you. Can you tell me about it? It might help your mother."

"Hey, you know why I like mushrooms?" Graham interjected. Ame shrugged with great anticipation. "Because I'm a fun-guy."

Ame roared with laughter, and gave him a high five.

"Good one, older than the mold in your underwear, but still classic. You know I'm missing my mom, but I've heard absence makes the heart grow fungus."

Graham slapped his knee, and chuckled loudly.

Diana entertained another face palm. "Can you please not glorify the use of psychedelic drugs? They are psychological tools, not recreational candy!"

Ame let out an exaggerated sigh. "Jeez. I'll tell you about my trip already. I definitely wasn't trying to kill myself, if that's what you're thinking. In fact, I believe the Woman in Wool was trying to kill me. I saw her, and she looked the same as she did in the barn. She was young, but older than me. She was tall, a redhead and she was soaking wet," Ame said. She paced the living room as she remembered. "But before the ghost appeared there was a wolf, and he spoke with his eyes. He acted as if *I* knew the way to get somewhere, and I acted as if I did indeed know the way, but it wasn't time to go yet. When the redhead appeared, the wolf was obviously my ally. The Woman in Wool predicted Eli and I would turn our backs on my mother. I guess that happened when we found out about the paternity. This ghost doesn't like me. I'm not useful to her–in fact I truly think she wants me dead."

"I believe this to be true as well," Graham chimed in. "But you're stronger than her. I saw the look on her face during that trip, she was scared of *you,* G-Bread."

Ame and Diana silently stared at Graham... wide-eyed... in disbelief.

"Oh hell," he whispered. "I really was there."

Diana dropped her head in defeat.

"You were the wolf!" Ame cried.

Graham stroked his beard, anxious and confused. "I guess I was."

Ame spent a moment processing. It would explain the strange connection she had to him. It would explain a lot of things. "I remember Graham, or the wolf, telling me not to chase the Woman in Wool. I did anyway. I wanted to tear her apart, but she dove in the lake and it burst into flames. It was a trick. My consciousness shifted. I was running through a forest, carrying a bulky bag. I could hear a horse chasing me... whoa... easy does it there Granny..."

Diana was on the edge of her seat, and looked as though she might pass out.

"I don't see how this is going to help my mother."

"Patience G-Bread. I think we both helped more than you realize," Graham said.

"Most excellent. Perhaps I can sleep with both eyes shut soon. Can we go to the grave site now before I lose my nerve?" Ame asked.

Graham patted her knee, reassuringly. "Absolutely. Then can we go bowling?"

"Oh hell yes, G-Dizzle."

CHAPTER EIGHTEEN
Irvine, 2010s

Marcus entered the house on the hill late Thursday evening. It had been a long day on the farm. He felt nasty, full of dust and grime. All he wanted was a long shower, a cold beer, and to catch the end of the Cardinal game. He didn't want to talk mysticism and he didn't want to talk about his sister, whose unfettered grip on reality had been a family headline for way too long.

"Why didn't you just call me?" Marcus questioned his mother irritably. A dust cloud danced in the evening light as he removed his ball cap, and shook out his dusty hair–his ritual entrance.

"I can't reach Gretchel or Eli by phone. Do you know where they're staying?" Ella asked, as she paced the kitchen.

"No, and I don't care. They're on vacation, right? Just leave them alone. Maybe their phones died and they didn't take a charger. Gretchel said Eli's bad about having his phone off anyway. They'll be back soon, so just relax, Mama."

He was about to turn around to leave when he spotted a bowl of sugared strawberries waiting for him on the kitchen table. He shook his head at Ella... She knew his weakness. It had been his father's too. He picked up the bowl of summer goodness, and began scooping heaping spoonfuls into his mouth.

"I don't like the idea of Diana snooping around the cottage. The basement wasn't secured on Beltane, and I'm hoping Gretchel had the sense to lock it before she left. She has the only key."

"And why you trusted her with that is beyond me," Marcus ranted. He filled a glass of water and downed it in three gulps.

"I don't want that *woman* down there finding things that shouldn't be found."

"Then march down to the cottage and kick her out!" Marcus suggested. Ella glared at her son. "Mama, the ghosts are already awake? What the hell are you afraid of, that Diana might stumble upon a way to *help* Baby Girl? Heaven forbid this madness come to an end."

"This is a delicate matter, and it needs to be treated as such! There is danger involved in allowing Gretchel to see things she isn't ready to see!" Ella roared. She paced across the kitchen again, and then spoke softer, almost to herself. "Diana cannot be allowed to uncover secrets before their time. My gut is telling me something's already happened. Why would Gretchel leave town so suddenly without telling us? I can sense that something else is going to happen too. Something she's not ready for. I can sense it with every bone in my body."

"Oh Christ, Mama! It's been what, twenty-five years? How long is it going take her to be ready? We can't watch her every dad gum minute, and I'm sick and tired of trying. Let Eli and his parents have a turn baby-sitting."

Ella snatched the bowl of strawberries out of his hand. "You're a big tough guy when Baby Girl's not around Marcus Bloome, but if she were here you'd be melted butter."

"Well she isn't here, so let me enjoy the hiatus! I'm busting my ass trying to run this farm. Can you just gimme a break?"

Ella ignored him, and kept pacing. "Has Ame been acting funny to you, like she's keeping something from us?"

"Ame always acts funny Mama, that's her nature. She's just like Gretchel: unpredictable and ferocious. Please quit worrying. In fact, if you're so concerned about Diana being at the cottage and the basement door being locked, why don't you show a little common courtesy and invite Graham and Diana over for an evening? Let Grand Mama them a story or two. Give Diana what she wants. That should keep her occupied while you find a way to secure the basement."

Ella considered the idea. She had to admit that it could work. Then her mind began obsessing over her daughter's fate again.

"Marcus, when was the last time you spoke to Devon?"

"Oh no. No way. I'm not going there, Mama!" Marcus hollered, and smacked his hat against the countertop. A cloud of dust exploded between them.

"Do you have all the guns in the safe?"

"Mama, stop it! I'm too damn tired to go 'round in

circles tonight, and unless you want to fill me in on what the hell you and Grand Mama have up your sleeves, I don't want to hear another word."

"You don't need to know yet. Gretchel has to be ready to tell her story before anything else about the prophecy is revealed."

With both hands, Marcus pulled the ball cap back on his head as hard as he could, practically making it a visor. "Well good luck with that," he stated and charged out the door.

∞

Ame wandered around the graveyard looking at the various dates and names. Stopping in front of a weathered old block of a headstone, she closed her eyes and held out her hands. She was being called to bear witness. She received a psychic download. She saw a woman's life story very clearly. *It had ended in sickness. It was a terrible coughing sickness. At one time the woman was vibrant, creative and well known for her dressmaking skills. She slipped away with her large, grieving family by her side. There was a dress hidden in a closet. It was red velvet, with extraordinary embroidery. She wanted her great, great granddaughter–in design school–to have the dress.*

Ame stepped back and shook out her arms. It was the second time she'd experienced such a transaction.

"Genevieve, your granddaughter will have that dress. I'll see to it," she whispered to the spirit.

Ame quickly, slightly on edge, continued through the gravesite. She would have much rather been a witness to the spirits all day long than to do what she came here to do. She was feeling mixed emotions as she meandered through the maze of stones.

She finally approached Troy's grave, and blew out a disbelieving snort. She shook her head, and looked up at the sky, after reading the epitaph Beatrice Shea–the woman she believed was her grandmother–had inscribed on Troy's headstone: *Cherished Son. Loving Husband. Devoted Father.*

"Fucking diabolical," Ame spat.

"What's that, darling? Do you need some space? Would you like us to leave?" Diana asked.

"No. I'd like you to stay next to me. This is going to be very hard. I may lose my shit," she said through a dry sob and a weak grin. She sat down. Graham and Diana immediately sat down on either side of her, and each took a hand.

It took Ame several minutes before she could begin. "Hey jerk. I guess you knew I wasn't your kid. I guess you always knew," she started in a soft tone. She picked at the spring grass. It had just started to turn from brown to bright green. She mindlessly tossed a handful at the stone.

And then she began to sob.

"It wasn't fair!" she screamed. She clawed at the earth, and threw chunk after chunk of dirt clods toward Troy's grave.

Graham and Diana both waited for the sobs to calm. Then Graham lightly stroked Ame's hair, and Diana rubbed her back. Neither spoke.

Diana understood why Ame wanted to do this with people she barely knew. It would be too hard with anyone else. This way she was able to let go completely, and still have support. She should have known her granddaughter would be so perceptive.

"You were such a horrible human being. You were the most plastic person I've ever known. You were ruthless and abhorrent. The things you did to us were atrocious. You were the psychopath next door. You are the epitome of hatred, and the poster child for suburban evil. How could you do the things you did? What kind of man beats his children, and then smiles moments later? What kind of man intends to rape a sixteen-year-old girl in her own bedroom? What kind of man beats a little girl who couldn't defend herself? You're no man. You're a coward and a fraud! How could you?" Ame bellowed. She pulled more clumps from the moist ground and launched them repetitively at the stone.

"Fuck you for ever laying eyes on my mother. Fuck you for what you did to Zach. Fuck you for fooling everyone. Fuck you for taking my mother away from her family. Fuck you for damaging her. Fuck you for stealing my mother away from me as a child. Fuck you for existing. Fuck you. Fuck you. Fuck you. You fucking fuck!"

Ame cursed and littered the gravestone with mud, grass, spit and disdain until the fight was drained from her being. She was elbow deep in dirt. Her face was a dirty map of random tear tracks.

She collapsed in Graham's arms, and continued to sob.

"You jerk. I hate you so much," Ame said hoarsely and threw her wad of tissue at the marker. It sailed weakly toward the stone, and then dropped quickly to the pile of thrown dirt. "But I forgive you."

Diana's head snapped to Graham's and they both shared a shocking understanding.

"I forgive you Dad–or Troy–whoever the hell you are. I forgive you. I forgive you for hating me, for resenting me, for whipping me, for locking me up, for beating me, for constantly sabotaging me. I forgive you. I forgive you for what you intended to do to me on New Year's Eve. I forgive you for destroying my mother and stealing her spirit. I forgive you for guiding Zach in the wrong direction. I forgive you for lying and cheating your way through life. I forgive you. I forgive you for everything," she cried. "I can't say it won't take me a while to get over it. All I can say is *right now* that I forgive you, if only for this moment. My load is heavy, and I have to rid myself of something, and my bitterness toward you seems to be the best choice... *right now*. You're gone, and you can't physically hurt us anymore. And I forgive you. But just for right now."

Nothing is unforgivable, Graham and Diana both thought to themselves as they eyed each other behind Ame's bent head. *Nothing is unforgivable, and this child is proof.*

"And I thank you," she started and then put a dirty hand up to cover her face. Diana was shocked, and she couldn't help but let out a sob of her own. "I thank you for teaching me to want more. I thank you for doing your job here. You served your purpose. I know it couldn't have been easy for you. I thank you for doing what you had to do to help me grow strong and resilient. I thank you for hardening me by what's happened. It made me strong and will help me for what's to come," she stopped and looked to Graham, who had tears rolling down his cheeks. He gave her a comforting smile.

"Mom's going to be okay; I will see to it that she's okay, and don't worry about me. I'll have help. I'm not alone anymore."

Diana surprised herself by kissing the girl's head.

"I'm done with this stiff lecture–pun intended–but hear this Troy, and hear it well: If I find you in the next life… you better run like hell."

Diana threw her arms around the child, and sobbed into her neck.

"I have to go now because a little garden gnome with a precision cut bob is about to choke me," Ame laughed lightly. Diana let go, and grabbed Graham's hand. "You can rest in peace, Troy. At least for tonight, you can rest in peace."

Ame stood, Graham and Diana followed suit. "Eli once told me that nothing was unforgiveable, and he was very close to right," Ame said looking down at the grave.

"*Close* to right, G-Bread?" Graham asked.

"Troy was a Cub fan, and who can forgive him for that?" she asked, smiling through a swollen, tear-streaked face.

Graham burst into hysterics. The girl was a gem.

"Are you ready?" Diana asked.

"Go ahead. I'll be there in a few."

Diana nodded. When they were out of sight, Ame hastily gathered a handful of dirt from her stepfather's grave, packed it into a small leather pouch, and stuffed it into her jacket.

CHAPTER NINETEEN
St. Louis, 2010s

Gretchel had wanted to make a few more stops in St. Louis. There was more she wanted to show Eli: Union Station, the City Museum, the City Garden, and on and on, but Eli drew the line. He just wasn't leaving the hotel again, and that was that.

He had already thought ahead and scheduled a full day at the hotel's spa for his love, which included: a full body scrub, a wrap, massage, manicure and pedicure. He had the concierge schedule an appointment with a personal stylist to do her hair and makeup. She would be busy and watched over all day. To Eli's surprise, she did not fight the pampering. And as deeply as he loved her, he was in need of some solitude. He was in need of water.

He spent the day at the pool. It was therapeutic. It was his element. What he wouldn't do to be on his sailboat for an hour or two. He floated all afternoon, and thought himself silly. He was trying to sort through everything. *What in the hell am I going to do?*

Gretchel had warned him so many years ago that she had real issues. He had taken his chances, and never regretted it for a second. He only wanted to be able to help her like he'd been able to do with the nightmares. He had an irrational desire to fix her and get his beautiful, sweet, feisty, innocently-in-love-with-the-world Gretchel back. Still, he knew he couldn't competently repair another person, but the thought of her being institutionalized ate at his soul.

While Gretchel was in the bathroom dressing that evening after having her hair done, Eli spiffed himself up, and checked himself out in his Armani suit. It was classic Eli, and fit him perfectly, all strong six foot five inches.

He pondered Gretchel's behavior that week. She'd been distant, in her own little world. *Is this trip finally us losing touch?* he wondered. He cursed himself for losing faith. He ran a little product through his hair, and suddenly long white fingers were helping.

"Jesus!" he jumped.

"Mmmmm.... I think I'll take you hostage, Hermes."

Now she's in the mood, of course.

He turned around to grab at her, but was rendered speechless once again. In fact, he thought he might take her right then and there. "Oh my."

"What?" she asked, as she coyly batted her eyes.

"Gretchel, why do you do this to me? I swear you're out to kill me." *Damn it!* He clenched his teeth and fists together. "I didn't mean it like that."

"I know what you *meant* Eli," she responded with an icy tone.

"Let me look at you. You're gorgeous."

She turned herself around. "You like?" she asked.

"I love," he answered. "Anyone ever tell you that you bare a striking resemblance to Jessica Rabbit?"

"I think you're the first."

Her hair had shiny, defined wavy curls with a huge orange poppy pinned to the side in pure burlesque beauty. She wore a black, cropped leather jacket over a long silky green dress with a slit clear to the hip, revealing black fishnet stockings. Three inch black stilettos completed the masterpiece.

"You said to dress like sex, drugs and rock and roll classed up, right?" All he could do was shake his head. "Well as an added bonus, if I get hot, and I'm thinking I might..." she took off the leather jacket and dropped it to the floor. The halter dress tied at her neck and met at the waist, leaving her back open revealing the phoenix tattoo in all its glory. The dress clung to her firm backside, making Eli's head woozy.

"I'll take you up on that hostage idea right *now*," he said pulling her toward him.

She pushed him back. "Yes, but then I wouldn't get my other surprise, which I have so patiently waited for," she laughed. She grabbed a big black clutch and headed toward the living room flipping her hips from side to side. Eli shook out his curls, and shuddered. This woman was dangerous in more ways than one.

"Have you seen my hitter box?" Eli asked.

"Going to get high are you?"

He gave her a look. "Problem with that?" It had been a while since he'd gotten high.

Gretchel chose not to answer. She rummaged through Eli's suitcase and came up empty. She spotted his constant traveling companion. "You brought your messenger bag? Really Eli? You're more attached to this thing than I am my doll. Where did you get that bag anyway? It looks old."

"It was my grandfather's, the mysterious Dominic Duncan. Who did the doll belong to Gretchel?"

Her head snapped up, instantly defensive. A venomous tension filled the suite. "That's none of your goddamn business!"

Eli could feel his heart pounding solidly. He'd hit a mighty fine nerve with that one, and he thought best to let it go immediately.

Gretchel, finally tore her vexing stare away, and dug in the messenger bag for the hitter box. Instead, she pulled out a brown paper sack.

"Oh my gods," she said. She pulled out a sandwich bag of 'shrooms. "Deep-see diving," she said and a smile warmed her face again. "Is this the surprise, Eli? Why in the hell did you insist I dress up?"

"No!" he grabbed the bag from her. There was a note inside. *Use sparingly, and carefully.* His father had sent him with help. It had been in the tote all week. Eli was apprehensive. The last time Gretchel had tripped she ended up in the Wicked Garden. He couldn't do this with her alone. He needed someone to watch over her. He needed at least one spotter.

"I want to take them tonight, Eli. It will help me, I know it will," she said grabbing the bag back from him and holding it to her chest.

He pulled the bag back. "We'll take them, but not yet, not until I give you the okay."

She pulled the bag back. "Let me keep them until then, unless of course you don't trust me." Eli held her in his stare, until his phone betrayed him. A text. He responded, and then looked back to Gretchel.

"The surprise is waiting for us in the lounge. Are you ready?"

She stuffed the 'shrooms in her clutch and smiled. "Yes."

They walked down the glassed-in stairway hand in hand. It was picturesque, two very tall, very beautiful figures stood out like diamonds against the sparkling St. Louis skyline. Eli walked into the lounge first and spotted his surprise. He entered, playfully keeping Gretchel behind his back.

She grabbed at his bottom. "Elliot Duncan, shame on you for torturing me with your secrets."

Eli snorted. "Payback's a bitch," he whispered. "But let's not wax ironic right now, Gretchel, there's fun to be had. Your surprise is here, and raising all kinds of hell, per normal. Now just pay attention and see if you can guess."

She listened closely, and immediately sensed a familiar presence. *A psychic.* She sensed others too. *Friends.*

"So help me Jesus, I'm going to brain you! Quit mooching my smoke, Will!"

Gretchel's face lit up. She turned to Eli, and hugged his waist. *This is the sweetest man that ever lived.*

Part Three

Carbondale, 1940s

Penelope stroked the hoof of the great god Pan. The statue had been a mainstay in her garden for years. As a professor at SIU, with a strong background in mythology, she certainly claimed many favorite mythological figures, but Pan always took the lead.

As she lay on a blanket in her lush green garden, she stared up at the statue's burly presence and smiled broadly. She felt the touch of her lover's hand. It was rigid and warm. The deep lines and fingerprints told an unspoken story of legendary courage.

An American-Scot, he had been a Merchant Marine during the war, and had come to SIU with the intent of using his G.I. bill to further his already vast knowledge. Penny met him during a lecture she gave on *The Odyssey*. It seemed this man had been on a similar voyage. He carried the weight of many an aimless voyage, only unlike *The Odyssey*, the quests of his ancestors never ended with a loving reunion of wife and child. He had told Penelope as much. He had told her many things over their blissful weekend. And keeping with the theme of his life experience, she knew there would be no happy ending for them either.

It was Dominic's second night at the House on Pringle when Penelope felt the knowing. The handsome stranger–who was not a stranger, but her soul's mate–was going to be leaving her soon. As she gazed at the stars she was utterly heartbroken, and completely satisfied at all once. It was the greatest paradox of her life. She truly felt like Penelope from *The Odyssey*, but she knew better than to expect her lover's return. She was a wise woman. She could feel it in the core of her being–this was the end, but also a beautiful beginning.

She slowly turned her head, and saw him staring into her soul with eyes of the purest aquamarine. His hair was a wild bush of chestnut curls. He was natural, and rustic, and completely pure of heart. He may have been sea-bound for most of his life, but he was an earthy fellow. He was more Pan than Odysseus, but either way, he was pleasing and loving her beyond anything she'd ever experienced.

They had talked about everything: mythology, philosophy, travels, political science, the war, love and peace. So many diverse topics, except for the one topic that haunted them both: children. Dominic finally questioned her. "Why haven't ye had babies, Penny? Ye'll make an amazing mother."

The subject was sore on her tongue. "I'm unable to have children."

"Are ye sure about that, my love?" Dominic asked.

No, she was not sure. It was what her doctor had convinced her of though, and it was the reason her ex-husband left. But no... Penelope was not sure the doctor had been right, in fact she was pretty sure the great god Pan–this beautiful Scotsman–had impregnated her the evening before. She stared up at the bright full moon, and looked for a sign from the Goddess. A shooting star zipped across the summer sky, and they both gasped at the sentience. She had conceived. They both knew it to be true.

"He'll be a demigod," she said, and playfully smiled at her poetic lover.

He gave a hearty laugh, and kissed her hand. "He'll be a wordsmith, just like me, filling notebook after notebook with his visions. He'll be an author. A pioneer. He'll have a deliberate, free-spirited message to share in this world full of predictable woe."

Penelope's grin faded. "Yes. Yes, he will."

"What is it, Penny?"

She thought back to the past semester. A man had come to visit her on campus. Another Scotsman. Charles Stewart. He was gathering research on Celtic myth, particularly information that might be associated with a strange chaotic knot. He showed her a photograph. He wanted to know if she had ever seen the knot on a box.

She had not.

Penny shook the strange remembrance from her mind, and brought herself back to Dominic's aura. "It's nothing," she whispered.

"It's everything," he replied. "But fear not, sweet woman. Ye and our boy will live a long beautiful life free of pain and full of love. Mah sacrifice will protect ye."

Penny was momentarily saddened by the finality of his words. She searched his eyes and found the divine spark that seemed to remind her of all that was good about the world. She focused on it, and found solace in the sacred glimmer.

"Take care of this boy, Penny, and the Horned God will take care of us all."

CHAPTER TWENTY
St. Louis, 2010s

Gretchel couldn't wipe the smile off her face try as she might. Over the course of her miserable adult life, she had often wondered what had become of her dear friends from the House on Pringle. There were days when she longed to hear Patty snap at Will. And there were moments when she swore she heard Will's guitar strumming or smelled the everlasting marijuana stench of the chronic couch. Will and Patty behaved like rotten siblings, and that was why she loved them. She treasured these people, and for a short time they had been a cherished part of her life.

Now, they sat before her, grown, grayed and lightly wrinkled, though other than physical differences, it didn't seem as if much had changed. Patty was still busting Will's chops, and Will was apparently still mooching her weed.

Will was still skinny, and Gretchel thought it odd to see him matured. Upon seeing her enter the lounge, he giddily raced to wrap her in a strong embrace. He pawed at her bottom and playfully tried to get a hand inside the slit in her dress. She smacked him away.

"Will, get your fucking hands off of her," Eli said, and it was with as much manly authority has he could muster toward his old friend. He wasn't above cold cocking anyone who dared touch his... girlfriend... fiancé? He wasn't sure what Gretchel was to him. Soul mate seemed to be the best phrase.

When Gretchel finally pulled herself out of Will's grip, she promptly joined Patty in a stationary hop-a-thon. *Oh, it's good to have friends,* she thought. Friends that knew very little of your story, and loved you for who you were in the moment.

"This is my wife, Lucia," Patty proudly announced.

Patty looks good, Gretchel thought. *Strong, as always, and content.* Gretchel shook Lucia's hand. She was a beautiful black woman with a wild head of curly hair, and a conservative way of dress. Gretchel felt the woman's hand, it was kind and soft. *She's an intelligent woman, an air sign, who balances Patty's aggressiveness.* Gretchel could feel the vibes, just like she used to.

"And this is Ginnifer," Will said.

Gretchel kindly nodded to Lucia, and then her eyes met the woman who Will held close. She was a tiny wisp of a thing, though Gretchel could tell the girl was aware of her own strengths. And she had seen this girl before. She had long, shiny blonde hair, with tiny flowers intertwined within various loose braids. She wore a long dress of white cotton lace. Gretchel mused that she looked as though she just stepped off a Grateful Dead tour bus.... *and wait... I've had that thought before. I have seen her! She was at the party before I left for the dorms!* Gretchel thought. *And she was there when I went back after Thanksgiving.*

"Pleased to finally meet the infamous Gretchel Bloome. I moved into your room after you went back to the dorms. The energy in that room was... interesting. We never really had a proper chance to meet," Ginnifer said.

Gretchel was struck mute. She nodded, and then took the woman's extended hand. An electric shock bolted through her body, and exited through the crown of her head.

"It's very nice to meet you," Gretchel barely whispered.

In a large, swanky round booth, the party commenced. Four of the six boozed it up. Two sipped on sweet ice tea and coffee. Plates of local delicacies, including Gretchel's favorite toasted ravioli, were passed around the table. It was the grown-up version of the munchies. Gretchel was pleased with the company she kept.

Patty had gone on to earn a Ph.D., and was living in Cleveland. Lucia, a former high school English teacher, was now a stay-at-home mom to their two adopted children.

Will and Ginnifer still lived in Carbondale. Will had graduated from SIU. He had his own graphic design company, and did tattoos on the side. Gretchel couldn't have been more proud.

Ginnifer was indeed the psychic who had communicated with her across the wild party at the

House on Pringle all those years ago.

Ginnifer and Will were not married, but they had been together since their days at SIU, and had four children: three boys and a girl. Pictures were presented and exchanged by everyone at the table. Will's children were all beautiful little replicas of he and Ginnifer: wavy blonde hair, healthy pink cheeks and lanky little bodies. Patty's kids, a boy and a girl both under the age of five, looked happy and loved.

"Well?" Patty demanded. She looked to Eli and then to Gretchel.

"Well what?" Eli asked.

"Where are your pictures?" Patty laughed.

Eli's mouth dropped open with shocking realization, and his face flushed in an obvious embarrassing panic.

Gretchel was ashamed herself. She hadn't thought to give him any pictures of Ame or Zach. She quickly pulled out a flat wallet from her clutch and located photographs, which Patty quickly snatched.

"Oh my god, look at that girl! She's a goddamned giant like her mother!" Patty screeched.

"Filter Patricia... filter," Lucia whispered.

"Sorry," Patty said. She shot Gretchel a look, and then drained her martini.

"Let me see that," said Will. "Holy shit dude. I bet you bought a shotgun. On second thought, I can't see you knowing how to use a gun, dude. Red on the other hand, I bet you...."

"Yes, I know how to shoot guns Will, and so does Eli," Gretchel snapped.

Eli stole a glance at Gretchel. She set his hand on

her knee, and she quickly interlaced her fingers with his for support.

Will passed the picture to Ginnifer. He laughed, and then turned thoughtful. "Ame's got your smile," he said to Eli.

"She does," Patty agreed. "That big, old Cheshire cat grin you used to get when you were stoned and holding Gretchel in your lap."

Eli blushed, and squeezed Gretchel's hand tighter.

"Yeah... I can see Eli in your daughter, but your son... no way. He looks nothing like Eli," Will told Gretchel.

Patty, buzzing hard, leaned in with a wobble to whisper in Will's ear. "I knew that baby was Eli's. Pay up you little fucker."

"Oh no. No way, dude! That bet was canceled out after Eli hit the bricks!" Will exclaimed.

"So help me Jesus, Will..."

"You're agnostic Patty, quit begging the Lord for help..."

Gretchel shook her head and waved her hands over the table, in an effort to silence the bickering. "Hold on now! Wait a minute. You two made a bet on the paternity of my child?"

"We just wanted to see you two back together, Gretchel. Troy was a total prick. You deserved way better than him. Whatever happened to that frat fuck anyway?" Patty asked, sipping at a fresh martini.

Eli squeezed Gretchel's leg. She didn't care. She was tired of the lies and the secrets. "I was married to the frat fuck for seventeen years. He fell out of a tree in January and died from the injuries."

The entire table looked at Gretchel in shock, all but Ginnifer who quietly drank her wine as if the proclamation came as no surprise.

"Come again?" Will asked.

"Eli and I recently reunited, and we're living together in Irvine at the cottage. Before April, I hadn't seen or talked to him since that last Thanksgiving in the 90s. Ame, my daughter, is Eli's, but Zachary, my son, is not."

The table remained silent, until Will turned to Eli. "What happened to you anyway, dude?" Will asked. "Gretchel came back after break looking for you and you'd already split. No note, no phone call, no nothing. I should just kick your ass right now for leaving her. I'd never seen a girl so heartbroken. I thought for sure she'd wind up in the obits the next day. Then I get a Facebook message from you outta nowhere all these years later wanting to get together? What the hell, dude?"

Eli thought he might punch Will in the face. He was starting to regret ever having set up the event with every word Will spoke. "You don't have a clue what transpired, Will. And I recommend you shut your damn mouth before I knock it out," he snapped. Then he looked to Gretchel. "You went back for me?"

Gretchel nodded. She'd never told him. His heart sank.

Will looked at Patty and she gave him a shrug.

"Can we change the subject please?" Patty pleaded.

"Not yet. Allow me to clarify this once and for all. I'll tell you what happened, Will," Gretchel said with courage in her voice. "Eli did not abandon me. He's not that kind of man. I left him first. When I finally came to my senses, I snuck away from Troy and made it to the House on Pringle, but it was too late. Eli was gone. You all remember my meltdown. End of conversation," she paused to glare at Will. "If you mention it again *I* will kick your ass. Keep in mind that I do not make idle threats, and unlike Patty I sure as hell won't need any help from Jesus to do it."

Will chose not to test Gretchel's patience, and the evening carried on with dinner, laughter and reminiscing about the lighter side of their Carbondale experience, but the longer the night progressed the more anxious Gretchel became.

"Are you all right?" Eli asked her as she came out of the ladies room and into a dark hallway.

"I'm fine, Eli. No voices. No problems. This was wonderful. Really. You did a lovely thing. It was so good to see them and remember the most beautiful period of my life, but I'm ready to take the 'shrooms now. I'm not afraid. I'm ready, and I have you to guide me."

Anxiety ripped through Eli's entire being. He'd heard that before. "We have all weekend Gretchel, we don't have to take them tonight."

"But I'm ready tonight. I'm ready right now. Patty is about to pass out. Will's stoned out of his gourd, and Ginnifer won't quit staring at me. It's annoying. Let's just go back to the room. We'll see them tomorrow."

Eli shook his head in reluctant agreement, kissed her forehead and let her walk back to the lounge alone. He leaned against the wall, and sighed.

"She's not well."

Eli jumped. He clenched his fists, and looked deep into the shadow of the hallway. Ginnifer stood tiny and ethereal in her white dress. He exhaled and slumped against the wall in relief. "No, she's not well."

He had lived with Ginnifer at the House on Pringle for three months. He knew she was a powerful psychic, but he also remembered her being very standoffish, and keeping very much to herself. Her constant staring was creepy. That had not changed.

There was a long pause. "She thinks the 'shrooms will help?"

"Well, somebody does. I've seen the experience heal people. My grandmother researched the subject in depth. I've tripped an ungodly amount of times, but I don't know enough about guiding someone who is sick into the labyrinth. I'm scared, because she tripped once before, and I lost her along the way."

"Yes, but you know more now. You should try again. I'll go with you. I'll help."

"I want to trip with her this time, but I need a spotter. She's dangerous Gin, very dangerous. She is very capable and sometimes convinced that she should harm herself or others. She's not always in her right mind. She needs to be watched by someone with clarity, and I apologize, but I really don't think Will's qualified right now."

"Give Will what pot you have, and *I'll* be your spotter."

"Done," Eli said, and stuck the full hitter box in her hand. "You told Gretchel the vibe in her room on Pringle was *interesting*, what did you mean by that?"

"*Interesting* was a misleading word. The whole

house was a living entity. I've never in this life felt such a peaceful, rambunctious, loving energy as I did my two years on that property, especially Gretchel's room, but then I felt a lot of things in there."

"Explain?"

"It had the same energy I just spoke of, but there was also an enigmatic heartache. She'd started to let go of something while she lived there, and the energy remained in the room for quite some time. I felt a child too. I always felt the presence of a child."

Eli's heart skipped a beat. "A child? What do you mean by *that*?"

"A girl; age undetermined."

Eli groaned, and then considered the possibilities. It had been *his* room as a child when his family would visit his grandmother. That could have been the vibe Ginnifer felt, or it could have been the pregnancy with Ame, or it could have been... No! Eli just couldn't imagine Gretchel giving birth before Ame. She would have told him by now.

"Gretchel was in an accident?" Ginnifer asked. Eli shook his head *yes*, and wondered just how much she knew. "The child I felt was in the accident too. She didn't survive. The child was looking for Gretchel while she was in Carbondale. She was looking for a way out, and something or someone in that house knows where the gateway is. This child wants to be set free. My guess is that Gretchel is keeping her memory locked away in the recesses of her mind, either by her own volition or by force."

Eli was wide-eyed. *The missing descendant. No! It just can't be.* He was still convinced that Gretchel would have told him. Then he forced himself to believe the obvious. She wouldn't have told him. *She wouldn't have.*

"I never told you this Eli, but when I first saw Gretchel at her going away party, I saw a beautiful aura of light surrounding her. Our eyes met briefly, and she knew I was psychic. We said hello to one another telekinetically and then went on our way. I watched her all night. When she danced for you, the light grew brighter and brighter. She was pregnant with your child then. It was probably the most powerful energy I've ever witnessed. Just imagine how she'd radiate if she healed completely."

Eli clutched at his chest, remembering and projecting.

"The only other time I saw her was when she came back after Thanksgiving and you were gone. She was out of her head and distraught. The aura surrounding her was the other end of the spectrum. I could feel and hear a malevolent energy so profound I had to go into the backyard just to keep from sobbing and letting it infiltrate my mind. There was blackness in her heart, yet something was protecting her from completely going over the edge. I assume it was the charmed amethyst necklace she was wearing. I could feel its energy as soon as she walked in, but it wasn't radiating her essence completely, at least not at that point."

"She'd only had the amulet on for a few days," Eli whispered.

"Randomness isn't a part of my world, Eli. Gretchel came into my life for a reason, and I am more than willing to aid in her recovery."

"What did she start to let go of when she was in

Carbondale?"

"I would assume she was coming to terms with the death of the child who was seeking her out. I'm not completely sure, but the energy in that house was healing her. If she had stayed longer, she may have let this go already. Brace yourself: there were a lot of men in her life before you, and I think she thought she had come to terms with a relationship she had with one of them. Does the name Devon Marshall ring a bell?"

"Devon," he repeated. *Devon. Devon. Old family friend Devon?* She'd briefly mentioned him on Beltane. He was with her when she shot the deer.

"Devon who?" a stern, pissed-off voice asked.

Eli jumped.

Gretchel stood before him with a hand on her hip. Eli glared at Ginnifer. The psychic could see a man she'd never met, but not see Gretchel coming around the damn corner? Picky talent it was.

"My friend Devon is a huge Graham Duncan fan, and I was just asking Eli if I could get an autograph for him. We'll talk about it another time," Ginnifer said and swiftly walked away.

Gretchel didn't remove her hand from her glorious hip. "You told her Graham was your father?" she asked, teeth clenched.

Eli shook his head. "No Gretchel. She's psychic."

CHAPTER TWENTY-ONE
Irvine, 2010s

Diana was beside herself with anticipation. Miss Poni had extended a rare invitation for coffee and conversation at the house on the hill. With any luck Diana would be hearing more stories. If she were extremely lucky, it would stories about Gretchel.

The short psychologist and the tall word-weaver entered the home with gourmet snacks and a lovely flower arrangement. It was the least Diana could offer their hosts for the evening. This was a rare opportunity to gather information, and Diana wasn't about to screw it up.

They were settling in the living room with coffee, lemonade, sugary treats and small talk, when Ella received a call. "It seems Cindy needs help with some bookkeeping. I won't be long. Carry on," she said.

Diana had no problem dismissing Ella. Not only was she still embarrassed by the Beltane fairy claims, but she also thought Ella to be too quiet with not much of anything to contribute to conversation. Miss Poni on the other hand was a talker, and the powerful matriarch. Miss Poni was the one with all the information, of that she was certain.

"That's a lovely ring you have on, Ms. Stewart," Miss Poni commented. Diana smiled at the large chunk of lapis lazuli that matched the subtle tweed detail of her Chanel blazer.

"Thank you, Miss Poni. It was a gift from Graham."

Miss Poni smirked. "Aye. The Duncan men have a habit of gifting gemstone jewelry."

Diana nodded politely. She looked down at Miss Poni's ancient fingers, and found the opening she'd been looking for. "Miss Poni, you don't wear any rings. Were you married to Ella's father?"

Miss Poni's smirk remained intact.

"Subtlety is one of Diana's natural gifts," Graham sarcastically explained.

Miss Poni cackled, and patted Graham's knee. The two had become bosom buddies over Beltane. Diana found it nauseating.

"Yes, Diana. I was married, and it was to Ella's father. Would you like to hear the story?"

Well that didn't take long, Diana beamed. "Oh yes!"

"You're easy to please," Miss Poni said.

"I beg to differ," Graham snarked.

Graham and Miss Poni both laughed madly. Diana gritted her teeth.

"We tease, Diana. Well let's just pick up where we left off, shall we? I believe we ended with my mama drowning. Well, there was an in betwixt time that we haven't talked about, and maybe it's not important, or maybe it is. Between the time that my daddy was killed and the time that my mama drowned was seven years. And in those seven years my mama drank heavily. Scotch. Always Scotch. She was numb, and she wanted to stay that way. It's not unlike the numb that Baby Girl experienced when she put on the amethyst necklace.

"During these strange seven years, Mr. Snyder moved to the cottage. He and mama no longer had to hide their relationship. He wanted to marry her, but she kept putting him off. I think she felt too ashamed for killing my daddy. Either that, or she was contemplating suicide, which was something I had foreseen since I was a child. I assume it was a little bit of both," Miss Poni said.

"Do you think she knew she was going to kill herself?" Diana asked.

Miss Poni nodded. "I think she knew her young death was inevitable. She knew the history of our lineage. Alcohol quiets the voice, but it will drive one to an early grave. The voice wanted to see her dead too. She couldn't win.

"In any case, during those seven years, Mr. Snyder taught me everything there was to know about the farm business. I think he knew my mama was gonna die, and I think he knew that when she went, he'd be following right behind her, heartbroken. And he did. He died of a heart attack two weeks after her suicide. He left me his entire property: 2,000 acres of lush farm ground, all his equipment, his money, and his house, which is where we sit this very moment.

"I was overwhelmed with grief of course, losing the only people I'd ever really loved, but I carried on. I had complete control of the entire farm. I was a fair boss, and all the men that worked for me gave the respect that I commanded. I would imagine a little of that respect came from the stories 'bout my ruthless daddy, though they'd never seen him. They were also enthralled by the occasional sightings of the ghosts that sometimes roam this property when the veil is thin. I knew there were whispers behind my back about odd happenings they witnessed in what they coined the *Wicked Garden*. And they all whispered like little schoolgirls about the redheaded spirit that inhabited the lake. It was then that I became known as the *Witch of Snyder Farms.*

"It never bothered me. I *was* the Witch of Snyder Farms. I claimed my title like a queen claims her crown. I was a strong woman with natural gifts. I could *see* things. I could heal with herbs and occasional touch. I was intelligent. I read and continued educating myself with fierce consistency. I was feared and respected. When you are a young woman in a man's world, generating fear and respect is crucial to surviving, especially in my day. Things were different then.

"With the exception of my daddy, only one man ever got the best of me in all my years at Snyder Farms, and he was the man I married. He was a farmhand with big brown eyes and a flashy smile. He was handsome, well built and he infuriated me to no end. He was lazy and arrogant and the most sarcastic man I've ever met. Oh that man... he drove me wild, but the ones that drive you the wildest seem to be the ones you can't seem to get enough of."

Diana took hold of Graham's hand. She understood this logic all too well.

"Things changed for me when I met this strange

fellow. I could still feel the fire inside me that I had felt when I was a young girl, but I also started hearing the voice."

Diana let go of Graham's hand, and began scribbling madly.

"This voice was very faint, and lived in the back of my thoughts. Mama had warned me about the voice all my life. I knew it was coming, and I was strong. I had been able to hold the voice back, with few auditory visits, until I met this beautiful man. The voice started to come in clearer. It was confusing when she spoke, because she learned my ways of blocking her, and in order to get through to me she began to sound like my own conscious speaking. She was the one who convinced me, against my better judgment, to marry Jack.

"He was from the way of Indianapolis, come here to Illinois seeking work. It was the 1930s and the Great Depression had everyone scampering around looking for a job, not to mention food and shelter. He'd found his fortune at Snyder Farms. But he was a drinker and a gambler. I should have known better. I just should have known better," Miss Poni said shaking her head back and forth. She paused for a sip of coffee, and then continued.

"I was just twenty-three when we married. I had Elphame at twenty-four. After I gave birth, the fire in me went out somewhat. I could still feel it, just not as intensely. Being a mother was an absolute joy. I wanted to give this child every opportunity to succeed. I wanted to do it the natural way: the way of the Goddess.

"I tried like hell to cultivate a new poppy garden so Ella would have a place to dance with me under the moonlight. But I couldn't get a single one to grow. I could bring in the best harvest in the county, but couldn't get a single poppy to rise.

"Jack and I moved from the cottage to the main house shortly after I gave birth. I seemed to be more involved in being a mother than running the farm at that point. Jack slowly took over my duties as head of the farm without me realizing. I was too in love with my little girl to notice the transition. I was too involved with cuddling new life to see that my husband was turning the farm to shit.

"I'm still quite angry at myself for letting the voice talk me into the marriage. I'd heard that normal little voice inside my head telling me he was no good, but the Woman in Wool's voice always had a stranglehold over instinct. She said he'd be the best I'd ever find to put up with wild heritage like mine, and gods only know why I believed her.

"Jack was jealous of the bond I shared with Ella, that was very clear from the beginning. I encouraged him to spend time with her, to bond with her as well, but he was distant, almost scared of her.

"He never beat me; he knew better. He was an alcoholic, but not stupid. He only whopped Ella once when she was eleven-years-old and got caught skinny-dipping in the lake with some of the farm boys. He never said a goddamn word to those boys who ran off, but he gave Ella a licking like no other. I wasn't there, but she showed me what he'd done. Like I said, he only beat her once. I hunted him down and socked him a good one, threatened to break his drinking arm if he ever touched her again. I was a big girl of course, and I think I got my point across, though not nearly good enough.

"Jack said Ella was a harlot messing 'round and tempting the boys. Ella was of course a beautiful girl, redheaded, long of leg, big of breast. All the farm boys *were* chasing after her before she'd even turned into a teenager!" Miss Poni paused and thought of Gretchel. "Beauty and sensuality is a gift, not a curse. Any man with honor teaches his son to recognize this sacredness. Your son understands this, but I digress.

"I trusted my husband, why I do not know, but I trusted him with the farm, and I trusted him with my daughter. He never degraded me or tried to stop me from raising Ella with the Pagan beliefs, and to me that was all that was really important. I loved that farm, but it was just a piece of land that would carry on without me whether I owned it or not, but a human spirit... Well once you lose your spirit you're as good as dead, anyway.

"Yes, I trusted Jack with both my beloveds. Mistake! It was Halloween or Samhain to those of us who follow the old ways. As you know Samhain is a sacred, yet dangerous time. The veil thins. Ghosts find their way out of the woodwork, and they reach out trying to grab onto life in hopes to bring themselves back. If you ever feel a spirit hanging around, you'd be best to ignore it, or encourage it to go back from where it came. You do not want what they are selling.

"Samhain was the day my mama, Carlin Fitzgerald, died so many years before. I was already on edge on Samhain, and I still am. The voice–the Woman in Wool– is very powerful when the veil is thin. Well on this day, I not only heard her, I also saw her. I was at the cottage, smudging the perimeter of the Wicked Garden when she materialized by the old oak tree. Her hair was flickering in the wind, and she had an evil grin on her face. She made a gunshot motion, and it scared the living daylights out of me. I knew something was gonna happen, something big, something bad, but I had to carry on. We had our annual party to throw.

"We'd always had a harvest party at the cottage for all the workers and their children. It was an event that Mr. Snyder had started before my mama died, hoping it would bring her out of depression. It didn't, but I of course carried on the tradition. It was meant to be a happy, gracious event, in additional to ritual. That night was a little different. Jack was drunk of course. It was the wee hours of the morning, and the last stragglers had finally left. I was looking around for Ella, but I couldn't find her. I'd seen her dancing earlier in the evening with one of our plowboys. They were all fond of her, but this one was the most persistent.

"I noticed a light on in the barn. I figured Ella was with her horse. But something just didn't seem right. It was too late for her to be up messing around. I quietly opened the door, and I heard muffled screaming. I peered inside to get a closer look…" Miss Poni looked to Graham for support, and he quickly took her hand. "Jack had his daughter pinned down to the ground, hand over her mouth, dress flipped up, trying to put you know what in you know where."

Miss Poni paused to catch her breath.

"I don't mean to be so candid about my daughter's attack. Ella knows this story must be told, and she knows this event changed the course of history. The funny thing is Ella told me much later that when she was dancing that night she'd felt the fire in her erupt. She'd never felt it before. She was thirteen, same as I was when I first felt it, though she said hers was more of a low burn... a simmer.

"Well anyway, Jack didn't see me open the door to the barn, but Ella had. I ran back to the cottage, grabbed the old shotgun, and well you can kinda see where this is going. The same plowboy that had been dancing with Ella had come back to reclaim a straw cowboy hat he'd left near the bonfire. He saw me with the gun. I made a motion for him to be silent, and he quietly followed. Yes, he was going to be a witness, and at that point I didn't give a damn.

"I opened that door and the plowboy saw what my mission was. He didn't try to stop me or dare say a goddamn word. Jack looked up, and he immediately begged for mercy, but I had no mercy for a man who was intent on destroying all the good that I had been given. I shot that son of a bitch in the head just like my mama shot my daddy."

∞

Ella slipped into the cottage, and checked every room for anything that might be amiss. She stopped at Gretchel's chest of drawers. She could feel a malevolent energy. The holy, ancestral Quaich had been dumped of its loose change, and sat askew. She steamed. She gathered the quarters and dropped them back into the cup. Then her emotions turned melancholy.

Scenes of her wedding day, drifted softly to the forefront of her mind. It was the day Miss Poni gifted her the cup. She remembered sharing the precious holy water with her new husband. She remembered him touching her face so sweetly, and then she couldn't help her mind from fast-forwarding to the night of the truck accident.

"I'd do almost anything for one more day with you, Walt," she whispered, as she rolled her fingers softly around the rim of the cup.

Breaking her treasured and tortured nostalgia, she brought herself back to the task at hand. Zipping through the rest of the house, she finally stood at the basement door and forced herself to go down.

Standing in front of the tiny blocked-in room, she shook with trepidation. The room held so much anguish, and so many memories. It was storing items that she hadn't laid eyes on in years. She sure as hell didn't want Diana Stewart in this room. Not yet.

As heartbroken as Ella was, she still managed to open the door. It let out a spooky creak. Boxes were stacked in columns of seven. Shaking fiercely, she opened the middle box, saw a photograph and immediately broke into uncontrollable wailing.

∞

Diana was not surprised that Miss Poni had killed her husband. Fascinated, but not surprised. Miss Poni looked as if she was happy to have confessed her crime. Graham refreshed her coffee, and settled in for more of the tale.

"After I'd shot him, the young farm hand that had witnessed the crime, kicked the shit outta that dead man like there was no tomorrow. I'd never seen such rage in a person. It was like he himself had been the one assaulted. Then he held my little girl with such tenderness that I wept at the sight. It was all I could do not to lose it, but I had to persevere. I *always* had to persevere. All three of us stayed up 'til dawn burying him in the Wicked Garden, and laying the overgrown weeds properly on top, so no one would be the wiser.

"About a week later, a rumor spread around the farm that Jack had run off with a young girl to the city, 'course *we* started that rumor. I acted like I was heartbroken, and I suppose I was in a way. I trusted the plowboy to keep my secret, and he did. That's not to say he didn't use it against me from time to time, but that's another story in and of itself. Let's suffice it to say that boy became Ella's constant sidekick. That boy was stuck on her like stink on shit. I don't know if he was really in love with her, or if he was just obsessed with keeping her safe. It was a lot of both, I suppose.

"This man had his own demons. He confided in me that when *he* was just a boy his mama left his alcoholic daddy and their four children. Apparently his daddy was a bit of a beast too, but worse. He told me his daddy did things to his three little sisters all the time; things that fathers just shouldn't do. He ran away from home when he was fourteen. He'd told his three sisters that he would find work, earn money to support them, and come back to save them.

He tried, failed and never recovered from that failure. Two years after he left home, after working his tail off on farms around the region, he had saved money, and gone back for his sisters, but his family was gone. He had waited too long. He tried to track them down, with no luck.

He wandered around the state, picking up work where he could. He was a hard worker. Hardest worker this farm has ever seen! Oh my heavens that man worked from sun up to sun down, and he never ever complained. I think he enjoyed the work. I think it sustained him, and kept his mind busy. He was grateful to have the paycheck, and needed to keep busy to fight back the demons in his own head. The work kept him sober too, 'cause it would have been very easy for him to just pick up the bottle to ease the pain, but he didn't.

"He was nineteen, and my Ella was only a baby at thirteen. I kept my eye on him. Although as far as sex was concerned, it really wasn't necessary. He knew he was a man, and that she was just a girl. He knew not to take advantage of her, he knew because he'd seen too much already. He stayed on at the farm, even when she went off to college at SIU. You see, I insisted my daughter be properly educated. Education was of utmost importance to me. Even if she came back to become a farm wife, it didn't matter. Ella needed to know what treasures and questions lay beyond the little walls of Irvine. Knowledge was what my daddy tried to keep from me, and I'd be damned if anyone was gonna hold it back from my baby.

"Ella would come home some weekends, and the man would be waiting for her. Every now and again, he'd take his old truck down to visit. They were totally committed to each other, and theirs was a mutual respect. It was beautiful, and I wished I'd experienced that kind of love myself.

"I say it was love between these two, and it was.

But I felt his hidden motives. This man was obsessed with keeping a little girl safe, but she was no longer a little girl!

"They handfasted when Ella was twenty-one, though I had a bad feeling about it from the get-go, and yet I didn't know why. He worked hard. He not only respected her Pagan beliefs, but also adopted them as his own, as Mr. Snyder had. He was the love of her life, and he took good care of her, but too much. Way too much. A woman ought to be free to feel things out and make mistakes on her own. It's not good for a girl to be kept too safe and comforted. It threatens her wildness. A girl's wildness is her most precious resource. A woman should beware of any man that makes an attempt at taming her wild. But that was how their relationship worked, and I had to mind my own.

"It was so odd to me because I was such an independent woman. I never burned my damn bra; I was the one that would take it off and find a way for it to help me survive! Anyway, Ella never did hear the voice. As far as I know she is the only one in my bloodline with that distinction, and I'd never been so grateful for anything in my life.

"Shortly after they married, Ella became pregnant with Marcus. He was a special child. Very special, and he still is. He was the first boy to be born into my bloodline since before the time of the Solstice Twins."

Diana's eyes flickered with glee.

"Walt, that was the boy's name that married my Ella," Miss Poni explained.

Diana nodded and casually looked about the living room walls, hoping to match a picture of Walt with the story Miss Poni told. But there were no photographs of the man anywhere. She found that rather odd.

Miss Poni cleared her throat to grab Diana's attention. "You won't be finding any photographs of him Ms. Stewart. It's for the best. To move on, Walt was so grateful he'd had a boy. Told me he meant no disrespect, but having a girl, a voluptuous redheaded daughter the likes of us would have just driven him mad with protection issues. Of course years later it did."

The kitchen door suddenly slammed, silencing Miss Poni. "Story time is over, Mother!" Ella spat.

Miss Poni dropped her head. "As I said. It's for the best."

CHAPTER TWENTY-TWO
St. Louis, 2010s

Lucia could no longer hold Patty back from tying on a sloppy drunk, and Will couldn't seem to quit flirting with Gretchel. They finally retired to Eli's suite. Gretchel was hoping they would be going there alone. It was nice to see her old friends, but she was done for the night. She was sick of tolerating drunken people. She was ready to take the 'shrooms.

She took off her leather jacket, threw it into the bedroom and when she turned back to the living room, she found five sets of eyes transfixed on her. She looked at each face one by one. They all looked like they were going to ravage her body at any second. She'd felt this so many times over the course of her life. She had an otherworldly sex appeal: sweet and salty, confident and coy. The sensual Aphrodite archetype naturally seeped from her pores. And she was tired of being ashamed it. She turned around, and doing so heard a collective gasp. The halter dress exposed her bare back, and the phoenix.

"Good god," Patty drooled.

"Time to go Patricia," Lucia interjected.

"I'll help you get her back to the room," Eli said, grabbing one of her arms and putting it around his waist.

"Night Patty. We'll see you in the morning for brunch," Gretchel called out, but Patty was seeing double and no longer listening.

Gretchel watched them leave, and suddenly Will was coming straight for her. "That phoenix looks as amazing as the day I tattooed it on this gorgeous body of yours." He took her in his arms and swayed to the music. "You are smoking hot, Red. You're the only woman I know who has gotten naturally finer with age. How in the hell do you keep this ass so tight?" he asked grabbing at her again.

"Running, lots and lots of running. Now let go of it or I'll perforate your fertile nutsack with my fingernails," she sneered.

"Still fucked up in the head aren't you, sweets?"

She couldn't help but grin. "Worse than before Will, worse than before." He spun her around. "And that still gives you no right to touch me inappropriately. Do it again and I'll clean your clock."

Will's grin faded. "I'm sorry."

"I'm not," Gretchel retorted.

Eli came back into the suite to see Gretchel dancing with someone else *again*. He was happy and jealous all at once. He sat down on the sofa next to Ginnifer, who watched the dance with indifference. In fact it appeared as if she was looking right through them.

"Ginnifer." Eli ventured a tap on the shoulder.

She jerked, and not missing a beat gave Eli a pop

quiz.

"Did you used to sleep with Gretchel at the House on Pringle?" she asked.

"Yes. It was my room there when I was a child. My father owns that house."

"Ah, yes. I see that now. Your father was raised there too?"

"Yes. And I did sleep in that room with Gretchel every night until she left. She had nightmares, and my presence would calm them. It still does."

Ginnifer considered the new information. "I think the spirit child was waiting for you to come back too. This child saw you in a vision many years ago. She knew Gretchel would meet you one day."

Eli pulled on his lip, and tried not to appear spooked. He was utterly confused as he tried to piece together the wicked puzzle. Ah! But then he remembered something… Holly had channeled someone on Beltane while she was smudging the property. *You're the one I saw in my vision. You look just like I imagined. She should have stayed home like I told her.* It had to have been the child Ginnifer sensed.

"I'll stop talking. I don't want to alarm you before your trip. Speaking of which, you should really take the 'shrooms now if you're going to do it tonight. It's getting late," Ginnifer said.

Eli nodded. "Okay, we'll do this, but I'm telling you we are dealing with some fucked up psychosis. It's almost... I don't know how to explain it other than supernatural evil."

Ginnifer nodded. "The bitchy redhead."

"How do you know?"

"I saw her clearly in my head when I shook Gretchel's hand. She doesn't like me all that much."

Eli sighed. "Join the club."

∞

"Do not leave this suite. Do you understand me?"

"I understand you, Eli, but if you don't get that finger out of my face I will bite it off, and I am dead serious," Gretchel said.

Eli knew better than to start a lecture, especially in their moody state.

"You should change into something comfortable," he advised.

"Stop telling me what to do!" she barked, grabbing the 'shrooms out of his hand. She stomped to the wet bar for water. *Water.* Eli remembered Carlin's hand grabbing him from the lake the last time she tripped. He remembered seeing beautiful redheads from deep beneath the sea when he'd last tripped with his father. And he remembered being on a ship… A never-ending sailing trip. He shook his head of the thought. He'd never been so petrified of water in all his life. It wasn't supposed to be like this. He wasn't wired to go against the flow of his life source. He began chewing a handful of fungi. He changed the music on his iPod to Pink Floyd. *Animals* seemed like a good pick.

An hour passed quickly. Eli and Will played guitar together like they had so many years before. Also mimicking the past, Will was stoned out of his head, while Eli was definitely starting to feel the 'shrooms.

"Where's Gretchel?" Eli asked.

Will chuckled a little. "I don't know, dude," he smiled absentmindedly staring at the patterned carpet.

Eli looked around the suite. The red hair was nowhere to be seen, nor was the little blonde pixie of a psychic. "We've got to find her," Eli said, the voice echoing in his head.

Gretchel was sitting at the edge of the bed. Ginnifer took on her role as spotter, but she, like many others was captivated by Gretchel's spell. She slipped Gretchel's high heels off and let them lightly drop to the floor. Her graceful, little hands slid up Gretchel's thighs. She raised her hips. Ginnifer pulled the stockings down over her bottom, and slowly rolled them to the floor.

Gretchel noticed the sensation on her legs. She felt her body come alive with a wicked excitement she hadn't felt in years. The 'shrooms were kicking in. Time was slowing down. The music vibrated fantastically in her head. She could feel other vibrations merging with her own internal humming. She gently stood up, untied the halter of her dress and let it fall down to her hips. Her breasts were exposed. The psychic languidly took in the sight of her bosom, and then her scars. She flinched, closed her eyes and saw the accident.

"I need to change," Gretchel said, at least she thought she said it. She removed the poppy from her hair, and let it drop. The petals floated in slow motion, weightless in the air and collapsed softly on the carpet. "Can you unhook the little hooky thing somewhere down there and unzip me?" Gretchel asked her handmaiden. At least she thought she asked.

Ginnifer honored the request, and the dress slid off, revealing tiny black underpants.

Gretchel sat back down, and melted into the bedsprings, Ginnifer at her side. The merging vibrations were becoming stronger. It was an odd sensation, but not unwelcome. It was a mingling of synaptic impulses. Ginnifer watched her calmly. She massaged her scalp and rubbed her hair.

"Dude she's not in there," Will called, as they searched the suite. "Wait, here they... Holy Mary Mother of God."

The 'shrooms were either causing visuals, or Eli just walked in on Gretchel naked, and Ginnifer going in for a kiss. He grabbed Will by the shoulder and tried to pull him out of the room. "Get back!"

"Dude, where I come from that ain't no spectator sport," Will adamantly announced. He ripped off his shirt, and headed toward the bed.

For a moment Eli was speechless. His mouth was dry, and his mind was static. Then he focused on Will going toward Gretchel's naked body, and he sprang back to life. "Get away from her or I'll fucking kill you!" he bellowed to Will. "Gretchel?" Eli questioned. "Are you aware of what's happening?"

"She's on my side, Eli. She can see the Woman in Wool."

Eli looked at Ginnifer. "Did you tell her that!" he spat.

Ginnifer vehemently shook her head no.

"Easy dude!" Will said, backing Ginnifer off the bed.

Ginnifer grabbed Will by the hand and pulled him toward the door. "I'll be back," she told Eli.

"You think I'm a slut," Gretchel whispered.

"No. No I don't. That's nonsense and you know it."

She fell back on the bed and stared at the ceiling.

"The church claimed I was a succubus. I was sentenced to die. I should have gone up in flames. It was supposed to be me. I'm a worthless tart, just like Daddy said," Gretchel mumbled incoherently.

Between the music and the 'shrooms, Eli could barely focus his eyes, let alone his thoughts. "Gretchel, I can't deal with whatever it is your rambling about. I'm starting to trip my balls off and the last thing I need is for you to start degrading yourself."

"Remember tripping at the cottage?" she smiled.

"I do. But this isn't the same. Stay in the present; you've got to stay with me right here, right now," he said.

"Lay with me," she whispered. Eli stripped himself and slid into bed. They lay wrapped around each other. As soon as he touched her all his worries melted away, as if her white freckled skin was the antidote to all anxiety. The bed seemed to be moving, like waves on an ocean.

Do you feel that? she asked.

Eli was pretty sure he shook his head in agreement, as he rode the waves.

I love you Eli, please don't forget that... no matter what happens. I have to dance for the men now, lest I face a beating.

He could hear her in his head again–just like he had

when she'd tripped before, but he couldn't manage a rational response. He closed his eyes and found himself around a bon fire. He could hear the music, and he could see her dancing. She was so beautiful. So perfect, wild, and divine. The red hair flew all around, and her naked body twisted to the rhythm. Eli lay on the ground watching, awestruck. He couldn't move, and he couldn't grasp the loving cup she offered.

Eli what's wrong? she asked.

He couldn't reach the loving cup, that's what was wrong. Something was holding him back. He couldn't dance with her; he couldn't pull himself off the ground; he couldn't get up.

Am I not turning you on? she asked, dancing faster and faster.

What the hell?

He opened his eyes, and saw her distress. He was limp as a wet noodle, soft as a sponge.

"No!" he bellowed.

CHAPTER TWENTY-THREE
St. Louis, 2010s

It was a cry heard 'round the world. Will and Ginnifer came storming back to the room, and Ginnifer immediately climbed on top of the bed.

"Ah, shit dude. Are you kidding me?" Will gazed astonished.

"Get out, Will," Ginnifer warned. "I have a job to do."

"You're not jobbing him!"

Ginnifer was losing patience. "I'm a spotter! Go sleep on the couch, until I need you." Will shuffled back out the door.

Gretchel didn't reopen her eyes. She lay back on the bed, and looked as if she'd gone to sleep, except for an occasional jerk.

"Just calm yourself, Eli. I won't leave you. Gretchel's fine. She's right here. Just close your eyes. There you go. Now I'm going to put your hand in hers. It's imperative that you hold on." She covered them both with a blanket. He could feel himself sinking into another dimension, and Gretchel was nowhere in sight.

All he could see was an explosion of colors and flashes of vibrant light. All he could hear was water running. It felt like it was running straight through him.

Then the anxiety came upon him like the four horseman of the apocalypse–or was that just the music of the band *Aphrodite's Child* playing on the iPod that was stuck on shuffle? He didn't know. All he knew and all he could feel was fear speeding through his veins like he had been injected with hot lava. His body began to quake. He tried his best to keep hold of Gretchel's hand, but his head felt like it was imploding with raw pain. He held his head and curled into the fetal position. He was suddenly hyperaware of Ginnifer's soothing hands rubbing his back, but he couldn't let the comfort reach his heart. He was immersed in a bad trip, and couldn't turn around.

Shhh. Mother will return. She'll be back before you know it son. The voice was in his head. And then he felt the tiny fissures. His body cracked down the middle, and split open like an egg. His insides spilled out over the earth. They appeared to be globs of mercury, and soon he felt the separate pieces of himself regrouping, but as dual forces.

One part of him walked away from the other. He was in this part of himself. It was this part that now stood in a forest with a belt in his hand. He was using it to beat Gretchel. *No!* he called out, but he heard no noise. *No!*

And then he was his other self. He was dancing with Gretchel around a bon fire, sharing drinks from the loving cup. There was a full moon, and a drumbeat and other people dancing as well.

A flash of light changed the scene. Eli felt furry. With great alarm, he realized he was a squirrel in a tree. He looked down to the forest below, and saw a sheet of red hair attached to a young woman who was bolting as fast as she could move. Eli felt a presence. He looked to his right and a vaguely familiar woman with ice blue eyes and flawless skin sat beside him in the treetop.

"Gretchel needs help!" he squeaked.

"Aye. Ye can say that again, little one," the woman smirked. Her translucent wings unfolded, and she dove off the tree just as a black horse with a male rider went thundering past.

Eli couldn't remember how he'd gotten out of the tree. The next he knew he was his malevolent self again. He had just finished beating a man, and he was hoping he'd killed him. He would leave him there on the floor of the grove to rot for the ravens. With any luck the wolf that had been spotted that spring would eat the poor soul for dinner.

He wiped his hands of excess blood, and then spat down on the man. His victim moaned. Eli looked at the lad's face and gasped. He had been beating the messenger.

He *was* the messenger.
He was also very confused.

He lay beaten and broken as he watched a massive fire burn in the distance. He wept in the grass as a large snake slithered up to him and clamped his neck. *No!* He pulled the snake off and threw it as far as he could.

A flash of light and he was on a ship, sailing. The

harshness of the entire experience was slipping away. The horrifying feelings of despair were gone. He let go, and felt the grace of the Goddess fill his being. It was the same feeling he'd experienced at thirteen while he sailed with his father, 'shoomed up and blissed out, on the Caspian Sea. It was euphoria, it was rapture, it was new, it was change and it was good.

∞

What seemed like moments was actually hours. When Eli finally emerged from the warm womb of the Goddess, he stumbled around in his own head trying to make sense of his current place in the cosmos.

Eli, help me!

Gretchel.

He felt around his immediate surroundings, grabbing at starbursts and kaleidoscopic images. The voice was close, but still so far out of reach. A door opened and then shut. Then another door opened and shut. Then another. And another. A final door opened, and was followed by the sound of a large splash.

Eli was immersed in cloudy green-brown water, and he could finally see Gretchel. He might have been relieved if they weren't steadily sinking. He reached out to grab her, but in the slowest slow motion she shook her head *no*. She was holding a box with both hands across her chest, and wouldn't let go.

∞

Gretchel was drowning. She could feel the water

rush into her mouth, down her throat. *It was meant to be this way*, she thought, *and it's been prolonged unnecessarily. It's what I deserve, and this box is a reminder of that fact. It shall go with me.* She sank, and sank and sank, gripping tightly to a square, leather box. Doom was her only consolation.

The deadness infiltrated her being as the water seeped into her wafting body. It seemed peaceful. She wondered why she'd waited so long to feel this way? And what exactly was she feeling? *Was* she feeling?

Is there something I care about that is worth the pain, the guilt and the torment? Do I deserve this peace? Wait a minute. I don't think this is *peace; it's a false peace. Wait... This isn't anything! No. It's a trick. This is numb! This is numb again!*

A mad cackle rippled through the water. It was the Woman in Wool!

Gretchel searched, but instead she saw all her redheaded ancestors dancing around her in the water. They were pathetic, lost, drowned souls. She pitied them. They drove her insane and were useless in helping her find any solutions... But wait... They were behaving strangely. They were circling her again, but this was not to heal... This was to protect and warn. They were fervently pointing toward the surface of the water. *Are they trying to save me?*

Gretchel heard the Woman in Wool howling laughter again. With a nimble change of direction she held tight to the box, and with the other arm began lifting herself. She wasn't quick enough to heed the call to safety. The Woman in Wool grabbed Gretchel's long hair, and pulled her down further into the abyss, while the black-cloaked figure grabbed her arm and aided in the descent.

∞

The Goddess of Dawn tapped Eli on the shoulder. *Save her*, Aurora whispered.

Eli was still sinking when he heard a combination of running water and an ethereal plea for help. His eyes slowly squinted open in time to witness a trail of ghostly red hair move through the hotel window. She disappeared into the beautiful summer sunrise.

Gods, I'm still tripping, he thought. He fought to catch his breath, coughed and vomited water onto the bed.

The bed. It was empty.

He flipped over to see Will kicking at the bathroom door.

"What's going on?" Eli whispered.

Ginnifer rushed in the bedroom, and slipped a card into the bathroom doorjamb, wiggling until it released the lock.

Suddenly Eli was very lucid. He jumped out of the bed, pushed Ginnifer aside and saw Will attempting to pull Gretchel out of the bathtub; the floor was covered in water, the sink and tub faucets still running.

"No!" Eli bellowed. He wrapped his hands around her shoulders, Will grabbed her legs and they pulled her out and laid her on the floor. Eli began mouth to mouth and in moments she was spitting water onto the floor.

It's not supposed to be this way, Gretchel thought.

Just let me go. Just let me rest. She opened her eyes and stared up at Devon. *Damn him. Damn him for saving me.* Behind him she could see Marcus, her Mama and Grand Mama. They looked so upset. They were speaking, but she couldn't hear anything except the roar of the Woman in Wool inside her head. She knew what came next, and it filled her with a familiar trepidation. They were going to take her to the hospital again.

They should have let ye die. Ye deserve to feel nothin' after what ye did! the voice of the Woman in Wool blared in her head.

Gretchel blinked her eyes again, and focused on the face above her. He was talking to her, and crying. But these weren't Devon's eyes. And she wasn't a teenager. These were the eyes of aquamarine, the ones that had been foreseen. She knew these eyes so well. This wasn't Devon at all. *It's Eli, and I have to get back to him. I have to tell him what I've seen.*

CHAPTER TWENTY-FOUR
St. Louis, 2010s

Gretchel lay on the bed, swathed in blankets. Eli rubbed her face that was still cool from the water. Will paced the bedroom, and Ginnifer bit at her nails.

"Gretchel, please talk to me. Please say something, anything," Eli pleaded. She just stared into his eyes. He gave Ginnifer a harsh glare. "She never, ever locks doors. What happened?"

"The Woman in Wool blocked me out as soon as you let go of her hand. She got to her easily without your protection. The 'shrooms have the ability to get Gretchel where she needs to be to heal, but it's also dangerous because the Woman in Wool can get to her on her own playing field. The underworld."

"That doesn't explain how she almost drowned!"

"You were both thrashing all night long, Eli. When Gretchel finally calmed down, you did too. That's when Will and I both finally fell asleep just a couple hours ago. It's my fault. Hold me responsible, I should have stayed awake."

"Did you not *see* it happening?" he asked.

"I can't see everything, and I just said the redhead blocked me. If you had been able to stay with her I could have seen it through you. I had no idea she'd attempt suicide again."

"But you knew she attempted it before?" he questioned further. Ginnifer concurred with a shake of her blonde head.

Eli felt a squeeze on his hand. His head zipped around, eyes wide. "Gretchel talk to me!"

I'm okay, she mouthed.

"Can you try to talk?"

"My doll," she whispered.

Eli grabbed the old ragdoll and snuggled it into Gretchel's cocoon.

Ginnifer saw the doll, and flinched.

The reaction terrified Eli, but he dare not question her about the original owner of the doll yet. He was pretty sure he knew the answer anyway.

"I got lost and she found me," Gretchel managed weakly.

"The Woman in Wool found you?" Eli asked.

"Yes."

Will looked at Ginnifer and shrugged a confused look. Ginnifer motioned for him to be still.

"I'm sorry, Gretchel. I'm so sorry," Eli cried.

Ginnifer moved away from the doll, and joined an abnormally serious and quiet Will at the edge of the bed.

"It was horrible," Gretchel continued. "I have good news though."

Eli's curls popped up, and regained some bounce.

"What is it Gretchel? What did you see?"

"I know where the box is, but she doesn't want me to retrieve it. She doesn't want it opened, but it has to be opened, Eli. It *has* to be. You have to help me find it, and for the love of the Goddess, do not let her change my mind."

∞

Eli did not rush the matter, though he wanted to very badly. He'd heard his mother mention the box earlier that spring when he'd visited their Oregon home, before he reunited with Gretchel. He intuitively knew it was very important to the prophecy and to Gretchel's recovery.

He couldn't push her though. He lay beside her for a long time, while she gazed at him, and rested. She wasn't ready to tell him what she'd seen. She was too weak and psycho-weary from the trip.

He ordered room service for everyone, and showered while Ginnifer lay beside Gretchel. By the time Patty and Lucia were banging on their door at ten o'clock, Eli and Gretchel were heading down I-70 back to Irvine.

He'd given the suite to Will, and instructed him to tell the girls they would all meet up later in the summer, his treat again, anywhere they wanted to go.

Gretchel hadn't showered. Eli wouldn't let her get anywhere near the tub. She looked like hell as she stared out the windshield of the car. "Please hurry, Eli. I want that box in our possession. We have to get to it before she comes back to me. I'm afraid of myself. I'm afraid

I'm going to hurt somebody unintentionally."

A vision of the arrow whizzing toward his head was a stark reminder of how dangerous she could be.

He pushed the accelerator further.

"Carlin hid the box in the lake, didn't she?" Eli asked.

"No. Not the lake. Suzy-Q and Epona knew where it was all along."

Of course! Eli thought.

"Eli, before all the chaos began in the trip, before the Woman in Wool found me and I was sucked into the wrong door, something beautiful happened. I looked through a gateway that held the most beautiful scene I've ever witnessed. I can't explain it very well, but it was better than my idea of Summerland. It was a feeling more than a visual. I was okay, I was healed, I was home again and *they* were there."

Eli could only assume who *they* were.

She continued. "I was forgiven and everything was okay, but I can't get into the room. The Woman in Wool won't let me. I have to get back to that door, Eli. I have to get back to that feeling, and that place. It is a place of redemption and peace and love."

He felt the desperateness in her plea, and he wanted nothing more than to make her wish come true. "Sweetheart, I want that for you, but I don't know how to get you to that place. I couldn't even stay with you momentarily at the beginning of the trip."

Gretchel stared out the window trying not to let him see her tears. "The messenger can go anywhere."

"Not this one," Eli said dryly.

"You were forgiven too, Eli. I felt it."

What in the hell does that mean? he wondered.

Gretchel raked her fingers through the ragdoll's hair, and then held it close to her chest. *And* she *was there too… I saw her. Sweet Aurora.*

CHAPTER TWENTY-FIVE
Irvine, 2010s

Diana stood in the kitchen of the cottage attempting to cook eggs for brunch. She mindlessly knocked the mixture back and forth with a spatula, while she contemplated the new information gathered from Miss Poni. The details about Gretchel's father were huge. She heard Carlin's story, Miss Poni's story, and part of Ella's. Now if she could just hear Gretchel's story... Well then maybe things would make better sense.

She wanted to know who else was buried in the Wicked Garden. She thought about the truck and the accident. She couldn't imagine how painful Gretchel's burns must have been. *Wait...What's this? Is this compassion?* It was still new for her. Daydreaming, she could almost see the smoke and smell Gretchel's flesh wounds. It was a sickening stench. She opened her eyes and saw smoke rolling in the kitchen

"Oh shit."

I'm not a damn cook, she thought. *I've never been a damn cook.* Breakfast had turned into a disastrous lump of burnt yellow goo, and she was pretty sure the melted tip of the spatula had entered into the recipe. She opened the kitchen window, and tried to wave the smoke out just as Eli raced into driveway.

"Well, he's driving reckless," she said. She also noticed that the pair had returned early. "They're home!" she announced to Graham and Ame who were giggling at the morning comics in the living room.

Diana continued watching from the window. They weren't unpacking. In fact they both ran to the barn. "Graham, something's happening!"

They came running out of the barn with two shovels.

"What's going on?" Diana demanded, Graham and Ame behind her.

"We know where the box is," Eli said. He tossed his father a shovel, and led them all toward the Wicked Garden.

Ame comforted her mother, while the men dug relentlessly. Diana watched with anticipation. A very delicate circle had been carved around the blooming poppy and it had been pulled up, roots and all, and set aside under the oak tree, then the real digging commenced.

"I've changed my mind. I don't think I can handle this," Gretchel said.

Eli stopped, wiped his brow, and motioned for his father to hurry. "We aren't stopping!" he yelled.

"Mom, we know it's part of the prophecy. We need this box. Just chill," Ame said.

Within an hour a deep square hole had been dug. Graham was at ground level, catching his breath, when Eli hit something solid and heard a scraping sound. He applied gentle pressure, and with a swipe of his shovel revealed a white stone. With trembling fingers, he loosened the dirt until a hole was revealed... And then another. When the third, slightly larger hole was unearthed, Eli fell backward and scurried himself to the other side of the excavation.

"What is it?" Graham called.

Eli's whole body shook, not from side effects of the 'shrooms nor from fatigue, but from sheer terror. "It's one of the men," he was able to muster in a scratchy, parched voice.

Gretchel shrieked, and Diana smiled wickedly.

Ame shot an angry look at her grandmother, and held her mother tighter.

Eli gathered what courage and physical strength he had left and went back to wok
rk, though it wasn't long before he hit another solid formation. This one was in the center of the hole, directly below where the poppy had grown. Sure enough, the poppy had been a sign. It was the box.

Graham jumped back in, and the relic was successfully recovered. Ame crawled to the edge of the hole, and motioned for Eli to hand up the box.

Then there was a quickening. A supernatural force descended upon Ame. She fell into the hole, and landed with a hard thud on her bad shoulder.

Gretchel had kicked her in.

"Mom!" Ame yelled. Gretchel's eyes had gone cloudy, her lips parted slighted and her face turned beet red. She was kicking dirt back into the hole, onto Ame, with the clear intent of burying her daughter alive.

"Leave it there or I'll kill you both!" Gretchel growled, tone unrecognizable.

"You'll do no such thing you evil little bitch!" Diana yelped.

Eli clawed at the graveside, scampering to protect his love. "Don't talk to her that way! Don't do it, Mother!"

"This isn't Gretchel were speaking to anymore, Elliot. This is someone else, someone who speaks through her, but is no longer of this world, and I'm on to your game, Mage McPherson," she spat down at Gretchel, who still crouched at the edge of the hole. Within moments the light came back to her eyes.

Without taking her glare off of Gretchel, Diana yelled to Eli, "Hand over the box!"

Eli brushed the dirt off his daughter, and helped her up and out of the hole. He handed up the box and Ame had to pause to catch her breath. "It's heavy," she said, nearly breathless. "It's really heavy."

Eli hadn't noticed it being heavy, but it definitely had a troublesome aura. He'd be happy to let go of it.

"Can you take this?" Ame asked her grandmother.

"Of course," Diana said. She eagerly took the box, as if she were receiving a coveted birthday present.

"Thank you," Ame replied contritely. Then she turned to her mother and charged.

Both Graham and Eli grabbed the girl. It took both men and all their strength to stop Ame from reaching Gretchel.

"How dare you!" Ame screeched. The men held her, until some of her rage subsided. "I hope you didn't mean to do that, and I hope you didn't mean to shoot at us with that arrow. That demon inside your head has pushed me past my level of tolerance. Anymore bullshit, and I will beat her out of you myself!"

Tears rolled down Gretchel's face. She hated herself. She hated the Woman in Wool. She hated everything she was, and everything that tied her to the prophecy. She was not a murderer. She wanted to be gentle and sane and a good mother. She hated herself with every nerve in her body again and anew.

Eli still held Ame back. He could see the anguish in Gretchel's eyes, and it was killing him. He knew this wasn't her. He wasn't even sure who the real Gretchel was anymore. He only knew that the possession had crossed a new boundary, and she was becoming more dangerous by the day. He had only one priority now, in that moment, and that was to protect his daughter.

He looked to his father. "Watch out for Gretchel while I take Ame inside."

Diana smirked at Gretchel, hugged the box and followed.

Graham kneeled down next to Gretchel who was now sobbing. "Honeylove," he whispered. "You have to hold on to your true spirit. Hang on as if your life depends upon it, because I'm beginning to think it does. I will not turn my back on you. I will not leave," he whispered, as he watched the others escape inside the cottage.

Gretchel shook her head in acknowledgement, but she'd heard those words from the messenger before, and they cut her and the Woman in Wool to the very core.

∞

Diana treated the box as if it were an infant. She sat at the old farm table, and took her time delicately wiping it clean. The leatherwork was the most intricate she had ever seen. It's knot seemed almost impossibly crafted. She had seen and studied many Celtic designs in her work as a mythologist, but she had never come across one so chaotically organized. It was baffling.

"Why is it so dense?" Ame asked. She watched with intrigue as Diana worked on the box.

"It didn't seem that heavy to me," Diana replied. She considered Ame's reaction. "Darling, can you touch the box? Just lay your hand on top of it and tell me what you sense."

Ame placed her hand on top of the box, palm in the center of the knot and paused. "It has a very strong energy. I feel pressure. It's a heavy pressure and I'm not even holding it. It wants to be opened. I can feel that for certain," Ame closed her eyes and her face contorted as if she suffered. "Now I feel heartache and pain. Incredible pain."

Ame retreated. Diana cautiously touched the box. She felt nothing, but disdain and animosity. *I don't understand. Have I become resentful toward the prophecy and this quest?*

"You look angry."

Diana pulled her hand away. "Well, I'm not. This box is proof that we all get what we deserve."

Eli brought their suitcases into the master bedroom, where Graham was attempting to calm Gretchel. "Dad, we took those 'shrooms last night and it was bad. She needs rest and watched over."

"Quit talking about me like I'm not in the room," Gretchel snapped.

"Then start acting like a fucking human being!" Eli snapped back.

"Quit degrading me!" she cried.

"You tried to kill me and my daughter!" Eli flung the suitcases against the wall in utter frustration. He regrouped, and went to Gretchel, putting his hands on her distraught face. "Just lay down. Sleep for a while. You *need* the rest," he said, and kissed her lips. He forced himself to act like she wasn't to blame for her recent actions.

She stripped down to her underpants. The long red tresses covered her breasts as she pulled on a clean camisole. Graham's eyes did a naughty eyebrow dance as he tried not to stare at the obvious goddess that stood before him. Eli cleared his throat. "Gretchel, could you please use the fucking bathroom. My father is right here," Eli glared at Graham, "…and he's a well-known pervert."

"Hey! I'm just a red-blooded male. Descendant of the Great God Pan…"

"Knock it off!" Eli shouted. Saint Elliot had reached his limit. He had dealt with enough insanity and dismissive behavior to send him over the edge.

Gretchel stared at her chest of drawers. "Who messed with my loving cup?"

Graham gave a wide-eyed secret headshake to Eli,

who clenched his fists in silent outrage. He would deal with his mother's snooping later. He intentionally ignored Gretchel's question, flipped back the quilt and pointed for her to get in. She did not argue, but her eyes told him she wanted to.

Eli reminisced as she settled into bed. She looked like a ginger-headed Rapunzel. Her tresses stretched across the pillow, and spilled over the mattress, practically reaching the floor. He gently cupped the red strands, and ran his hand through the whole length. The hair was such a sacred part of Gretchel's identity. And it still smelled of strawberries; always of strawberries.

He inhaled a large whiff, and thought of easier times. They were few and far between, but they had existed, and he was looking forward to a day when they would put all this weirdness behind them.

She sheepishly grinned at him, which he responded to with a light kiss on the forehead. Then he looked sternly at his father. "Make sure she stays put, and *do not* get her excited."

"What do you take me for, an incubus?" he asked, kicking off his Birkenstocks and sitting on the bed.

"He said I was a succubus," Gretchel whispered.

"Who said that?" Graham and Eli both demanded in unison.

Gretchel closed her eyes, and fell asleep.

Eli groaned, rubbed at his stubbled face, and stomped into the dining room where Ame and Diana were messing with the box. Diana looked perplexed. She studied the cube. There was no lock, there was no keyhole, and there were no hinges.

"I fear this box is charmed," she mumbled.

Oh, of course it is, Eli thought, and felt shamefully self-righteous with his defeatist attitude. He pulled a chair up to the table, and decided it was time to give away whatever it was he had left. "Grab a notebook, Mother. I've got lots of new material for you, though some of it is rather dated."

CHAPTER TWENTY-SIX
Irvine, 2010s

Eli began with Gretchel's twenty-first birthday; the night Ame was conceived. He shared the entire trip in detail, as Diana recorded the testimony. He explained how the ghost of Carlin Fitzgerald grabbed his hand; how he and Gretchel could hear each other's thoughts, and how Gretchel had wound up in the truck, and was filthy as if she had been digging or covered in dirt. He explained the vision he had on the lake of Gretchel wearing the exact dress that now hung in her closet. In the vision Gretchel mentioned that *'she wasn't afraid, that she had Eli there to guide her.'*

He told Diana about the trip he'd taken with his father when he saw beautiful redheaded sirens doing a ghostly water ballet. He explained the situation when Gretchel choked him before the Beltane celebration. He told her about his visions of Gretchel dancing, of the snake and the water. He told her about the trip he had taken just the night before in St. Louis, and Gretchel's attempted suicide. He told her about Ginnifer's reading, including Devon Marshall, a man Gretchel was supposedly involved with when she was younger.

Diana listened objectively. She was dumbstruck for perhaps the first time in her life.

"Why did you never tell me any of this before, Eli? Why did you wait?"

"For one thing, it was none of your business. For another, I didn't trust you or the prophecy. Now I'm at the mercy of both. You have to help us. You have to help *her*," he demanded and pleaded all at once. Ame moved beside him and rubbed his back for support.

Diana sighed. "She needs medication, she needs extensive therapy, she needs to be locked up, but how can that happen right now when so much is at stake? We need her to help fulfill this prophecy. How can I be the one to cage her when I'm the one that was sent here to help set her free? I'm putting my ethical ass on the line by allowing her to carry on this way. I could lose all I've worked for."

"This prophecy *is* all that you've worked for!" Eli roared. "It's not just to prove that mythic archetypes exist in reality. This prophecy is, and always has been, your baby, your obsession. Even Grandpa Stewart saw the mania it invoked in you. It worried him, probably to death," Eli spat. Diana gasped at her son's audacity. "And at what point have you ever lived an ethical life, Mother? Why start worrying about it now?"

The boy's got a point, Diana thought.

"She needs an exorcist," Ame mumbled.

Diana and Eli both turned to the young girl. "Yes. Yes she does, or an exorcism. Perhaps that's what will happen in the underworld."

Eli rolled his eyes and slammed the table with his fist. "Can we get back to reality?"

It was just enough to set Diana on fire. "Reality? You are in love with a possessed witch! What do you think reality is to her, Eli? What exactly is reality to you? You've seen the signs! You've witnessed the behavior! Are you going to sit there and tell me this prophecy is bullshit after everything that you've been through with that girl?" Diana yelled. "Stop denying the truth. A ghost, who is many centuries old, possesses the woman you love. Gretchel's had some kind of traumatic experience that changed her life in the most heartbreaking way. She's carrying the weight of that trauma, in addition to the trauma of sixteen of her ancestors! Seeing this prophecy through is the humane thing to do. As a Stewart I am loyal to my family creed: I will finish what I started. It's my duty to relieve her of this burden. It's *our* burden too, Eli! Can't you feel the call? I've felt this duty since I met the crone. I've felt a duty to something bigger since I was a child with a broken leg on the Scottish forest floor after being chased by a wolf that my parents swear to their death did not exist in Scotland. I do not *want* to help her, but I *must* help her. So you listen here buddy boy, you can either play it my way, or you can visit your statuesque redhead during visiting hours. They aren't going to buy the claims of possession."

Ame, who had never seen Diana so frightening, whispered to Eli, "Let's do it her way. All she has now is us, our family."

Eli grimaced. "Fine. So what are you looking for now, Mother? You have your damn box."

"And the Quaich," Ame said.

Diana shot her a look. *Shit.*

"The what?"

"The loving cup you keep seeing in your dreams. The one you can't grab hold of because you're a damn momma's boy."

"What?"

"What do you think the snake means, Eli? What do you think it represents? I'll tell you what it symbolizes: Manhood! You clearly look like a man, but Graham sure did a shitty job raising one that notices the nuts between his legs."

Ame pushed back her chair to give Eli space. He looked like he might blow a gasket.

"You bitch," he growled. "If I've not grown into your vision of a man, that fault belongs with you."

"Pffft. Blame me if you want. I don't give a shit. This isn't about me. You want to quit getting nipped in the ass by a snake in your dreams? Then let it swallow you whole. Let it take you away and let it spit you back out. Your daughter's been a team player, why can't you be? She found the Quaich which I believe to be an important piece to this puzzle. It originally belonged to the Woman in Wool."

"And had you allowed me to see the entire prophecy early on I might have been able to help locate it sooner," Eli said.

"You can't handle the whole prophecy. You're too emotionally involved. All I know is I still have stories to hear, a Horned God to reveal himself, an underworld to locate, and psychopomps to find before the goddamn Summer Solstice!"

Ame stood up, knocking her chair over. "Holly's a psychopomp!"

Eli looked to the ceiling. He was going crazy. He was convinced he was still a thirteen-year-old boy under the influence of 'shrooms on the Caspian Sea and had never recovered from the trip. *Is this my reality then?*

"Is that what Holly told you in the Wicked Garden?" Diana asked.

Ame shook her head fiercely. "She said we were 'all in grave danger.' Who do you think the *we* are?"

Diana let out a little sigh. "Who has been in danger, Ame?"

She considered the question. "Well, obviously Mom has tried to kill Epona... Twice. And she threatened to shoot Suzy-Q, so they are both psychopomps."

"Keep going," Diana guided as softly as she could.

Ame's face rumpled. "She tried to kill Dad... And me. We're psychopomps too!"

Diana laid a hand on top of Ame's. "We will do everything in our power to keep you safe. You have to trust me. Your father will not let any harm come to you. He may seem like he's weak..."

"He doesn't seem weak to me," Ame interjected.

Diana snorted. "Ame, if anyone ever tried to harm you, including your own mother, I have no doubt in my mind that person would have hell to pay."

Eli stared at his mother. He couldn't decide if he wanted to hug or choke her. Instead, he put his head on the table and tried like hell not to do either. He was losing it. The effects of the 'shrooms were kicking his emotional ass.

"Quit your damn sulking and look at these," Diana

barked throwing three sketchpads on the table.

She's gone completely manic, Eli thought. He raised his head, wiped his face and pulled the pads toward him. He flipped through the pages, shaking his curly head in disbelief. When he got to the third book, the hair stood up on the back of his neck, which had become a regular occurrence since he'd come to live at Snyder Farms.

"Look at the dates," Diana commanded.

1984. "That would have been shortly after the truck accident," Ame said.

"Everything is connected, and everything is symbolic," Diana replied.

He flipped through the sketchpad of Gretchel's self-portraits. The last two pages were the hardest to view. The first showed an image of her face immersed in flames, the last one showed her sinking into water, red hair floating above her head. A single word was written at the top of the page: *Redemption.*

"The Woman in Wool wanted Gretchel to die in the truck fire, but she somehow survived. Now she's trying to get her to commit suicide like the others, yesterday being her third attempt. Gretchel is living out the demise of both Solstice Twins. It is my belief that Gretchel threatens the Woman in Wool. Gretchel holds some intense power that she wants to see destroyed. We have to figure out what that power is. What can Gretchel do that would destroy the Woman in Wool's power? Why is she trying so hard to silence Gretchel? It is my belief that the psychopomps, including you both, will lead Gretchel to this redemption. And the redemption is dependent on this box being opened.

"I still don't completely get it," Eli said.

Diana pulled out a copy of the family tree, and began drawing random lines. "Gretchel is living out an archetypical pattern that was set in motion centuries ago. The Woman in Wool does not want her suffering to end. She lives vicariously through each descendant; this is how she is able to keep feeling the anguish she thinks she deserves. She does not want this cycle to end. It seems a sacrifice is also necessary to keep her alive. She's had more than her share in the past hundred years, and I'm guessing this is the most powerful she's ever been. Gretchel is the quintessential host, but there is also something about her that is kinking up the Woman in Wool's cycle. There is something about Gretchel that threatens this evil entity, and we won't know what that something is until Gretchel tells us her story–unabashed, unadulterated, the truth!"

A lost cause, Eli thought.

Suddenly the kitchen door flew open. Ella stormed in with Miss Poni in tow.

"What's happened?" Ella barked. "Where's Baby Girl? What have you done to her?"

Diana scampered for safety as Ella stormed her way. "Stop it Grand Mama!" Ame yelled jumping between them. "Mama's sleeping. She's fine now."

Ella rushed into the bedroom to see Gretchel resting soundly with Graham's arm wrapped around her waist. With trembling hands, Ella ran her fingers lightly through Gretchel's hair. Diana and Ame stood at the door watching until Ella glared at them and marched back out.

In the dining room, she pointed a crooked finger at Diana, as if to curse. "If anything happens to my child…"

Miss Poni put up a hand to block Ella's intent to curse. She slowly walked her daughter to the ancient farmhouse table. "Don't be throwing out any hexes you aren't prepared to suffer for. That's how we all got in this mess in the first place. Baby Girl's strong. She's always been strong. She had to be. She's also got the biggest damn mouth I ever did see, but by gods she knows how to use it most times. Now just sit down Elphame, and let's look at what's been dug up."

Ella looked down at the table and gasped. "Oh, gods!" she cried.

"I always knew I'd see this thing again. Gretchel knew where it was. I saw a vision of her holding it this morning. She was sinking. It liked to scare the daylights out of me," Miss Poni said, a catch in throat. She studied the box as hard as Diana. She ran a finger over the stitching and instantly pulled back.

"What did you feel?" Diana asked.

"It burnt me like a lightning bolt. I remember it burning me before, when I was a child. Mama was trying to open it using magic."

"Ella," Diana started carefully, "would you mind touching the box just once?"

Ella wiped at her tears and conceded. She apprehensively touched the box, and jerked back too.

Diana looked to her granddaughter. Ame had carried the box, without issue other than it seemed incredibly heavy. "Ame, could you please touch the box again?"

Ame touched it. She didn't jerk, but she did wince. "It's doesn't shock or burn me, but it's energy seems so heavy–oppressive."

Diana didn't understand yet. She moved on to other matters.

"The prophecy states that the amethyst amulet is the key that will unlock this box in the underworld. This family, including all the ancestors, will be set free from the curse and the Woman in Wool."

"Yes, Ms. Stewart. That is what we believe too," Miss Poni said.

Of course, Diana thought, figuring the two crones were hiding so much more. "Ame, may I have the amulet?"

Ame removed it from her neck, and gave it to Diana. The purple gem shone like a dazzling pool of violet under the light. Diana gazed at it briefly, and then looked back at the table. "There is no keyhole on this box. There is no opening for this gem to fit. Is there any insight you are willing to share with me? I am here to help you. I have Gretchen's... damn it! I mean Gretchel's, best interest at heart. So how do we make this key fit?"

"I cannot allow this to happen! There is too much danger involved," Ella cried.

"You've no choice in the matter, Elphame!" Miss Poni snapped.

Ella slammed her chair into the table, and excused herself to the kitchen.

Miss Poni raised herself up, and with the all her authority announced. "The jewel isn't the key."

Diana cringed and stomped her tiny foot. Graham had been trying to convince her of that too. *That's nonsense!* "But the prophecy says..."

"I think I know what the prophecy says child, and I'm telling you that the amulet is not the key!" Miss Poni said, shoulders strong and voice even stronger.

"How do you know what the prophecy says then?" Diana demanded.

"Because the ghost in the lake, my mother Carlin, has been whispering pieces of it to me in my sleep for over thirty-seven years, and I know that gem is not the goddamn key! If you could put your overwhelming need to be right aside for a moment, the truth would expose itself to you easily, like it wants to."

The room fell silent. Eli put a hand on Ame's back, as Diana looked down at the amethyst necklace that sat on the table. She studied the gem closely. It made no sense–the chain–the clasp–the amethyst itself... Then Diana raised her head. Ame was looking right back at her with a single tear falling down her face. Ame already understood. A warm wave of knowing washed through Diana's mind.

Ame. Ame. Ame. Ame-with-an-E. Ame. With an E?

"Ame," Diana whispered. "How does the first name read on your birth certificate? I mean... your proper name?"

Ame swallowed a sob. She closed her eyes tight and answered, "Amethyst."

The key.

The first and second and the psychopomps
will follow the Horned God to the underworld.
Amethyst is the key that will open the buried box.
When the spirits are set free,
all will be redeemed.

EPILOGUE
Irvine, 2010s

Gretchel had slipped into a deep sleep. The people that cared for her hoped that the extended slumber would aid in the recovery of her post 'shroom ordeal. Unfortunately it was having an opposite effect. She was crying. The tears tickled her cheeks as they slid toward the pillowcase.

She was devastated by the realization of what she had become and what she was doing. The events that had transpired since she removed the amethyst were stuck on obsessive replay in her mind. She was hurting people again–physical and emotionally. When would this cycle end? When would the gentleness that she knew from the House on Pringle return? When would she be forgiven for her transgressions? When would she stop hurting the ones she loved?

Never. It cannae end, she heard in her mind.

Gretchel's tears came faster. She squeezed her eyes shut, and wished to be free from the pain that bristled her soul.

"Just give me rest," she pleaded with the Goddess. She picked up the rag doll from her nightstand, and held it close to her chest that was saddled heavy with burden.

She felt a new sensation then. Her abdomen was burning with phantom pains, which was not uncommon, but certainly unwelcome. The conflagration was excruciating, and becoming nearly intolerable.

Aye. I can grant ye relief, the voice whispered wickedly.

Gretchel wiped her tears. "Relief," she begged.

Suddenly she felt herself rising up, but not of her own power. She looked down at the bed. When she had gone to sleep Graham had been spooning her like a seahorse. At some point Eli had taken his place, but still lay sleeping. Gretchel tried to reach her hand out to stroke his curls, but her mind and her body were not cohesive.

A pocketknife sat on Eli's nightstand. He had told her it had been a gift from his Grandfather Stewart. It was British-made, and very old. It was his favorite. Her hand clasped around the cold object.

"Relief," she chanted in a pathetic, diabolical mantra. She found herself tiptoeing out of the bedroom, so not to wake Suzy-Q, who slept at the foot of the bed.

She was already halfway to the lake when she realized she was no longer in control of her actions. And with the realization, the pain in her mind, chest and abdomen amplified. She dropped to the ground reeling in agony. "Relief," she cried.

With her one-word plea, she felt her body on the move again, and was soon sitting on the island's boat dock. The Woman in Wool had taken full command of her body during the darkest moments of the morning. Upon this repeat awareness, Gretchel tried to fight the domination, only to have a seething pain rip through her form if she even dared to relinquish sanity.

She was tortured into submission once again. "Relief," she sobbed. She lay on the dock engulfed by the pain. And while the agony did not subside, she was suddenly in control of her body. Looking up she determined why. The Woman in Wool had manifested. Wet, frightful and undeniably beautiful, the ghost hovered over Gretchel.

"I can ease yer pain," the specter said.

Gretchel felt her abdomen explode with a throbbing misery of regret. She silently sobbed. "Relief..." she mouthed and nodded.

She lifted her camisole.

The Woman in Wool gazed over the burns on the right side of Gretchel's torso and then the nineteen equal cuts on the left. "Relief," the Woman in Wool laughed mockingly.

The ghost used Eli's pocketknife to methodically slice Gretchel's skin. It was the twentieth cut.

Gretchel jerked in pain. The Woman in Wool knelt down and was nose to nose with her host. "And when will ye learn ther'll be no rest'n fer the wicked?" she declared, anger and rage seething to a boiling point.

Then she used the knife to hack off Gretchel's long red tresses. She held the hair up to the dawn that broke brilliantly over the horizon. "The first of many more sacrifices!" the ghost yelled into the nether. She tossed the locks into the water that rolled mad with waves.

Gretchel lay helpless, her body quivering with

spasms. And suddenly it felt as if the sun and the colors of the morn were burning her body. It was as if she was emulating a blazing blister of self-hatred. She could not take one more moment of the pain, the shame and the grief. She could only crawl the short distance to the edge of the dock where the Woman in Wool kicked her into the water.

Whit's fur ye'll no go by ye.

COMING SOON: BOOK FOUR

Go deeper into The Wicked Garden...

You've met Aphrodite and Hermes, the Horned God and the Cailleach. Let Lenora introduce you to more mythic archetypes with her monthly newsletter. Meet fellow fans and discuss the themes of *The Wicked Garden* in a virtual discussion group. And look for updates on forthcoming volumes in The Wicked Garden Series.

Whit's fur ye'll no go by ye.

www.lenorahenson.com

Made in the USA
Middletown, DE
10 June 2015